Small Planet

A big journey on a small scale

Mike Edward Evans

Written with the support of the
Supporting Men Society

MIKE EDWARD EVANS

Author and Electrical Engineer

What started out as a hobby is quickly becoming an obsession. Writing has given me a new purpose and teh story ideas are constantly flowing. I hope one day to be as popular as some of my favourite authors.

I dedicate this book to my family. Without their input and support this journey would not have come to fruition.

Please visit my website for published booke and up-coming ideas.

www.mikeedwardevans.com

PART 1

CHAPTER 1 – SQUIRRELS AND THEIR NUTS

Thursday, August 12th, 2010

"There is no way you can tame a squirrel and ride it, Ben!" screamed Rosie at the top of her voice.

Ben could barely hear her as she was too far away, and he was concentrating on stalking the squirrel. Ben was just 18, and the years of living in the wilds had made him quite the athlete. He had the body of a natural bodybuilder and the six-pack to go with it. True, living here didn't give him any access to any fast food, sweets, or even chocolate. He'd had never tried any of it. His parents had often told him about burgers and ice cream, but with no basis for comparison to the food they ate, he couldn't see what the fuss was about. He was used to vegetables, salad, and natural foods from the land. Rosie was much the same, super fit and quite the looker too with long dark hair and a slender figure. She was slightly older than Ben at 19, but that didn't give her any authority over him, or so he thought.

The sun was peeking through the branches above them, making it look like rays were showering down from the sky. Bushes and towering trees surrounded them, along with long grass and other foliage. There were no clouds in the sky that they could see, just a blazing yellow sun making its way to meet the tree line in the distance.

Ben got right behind the grey squirrel who was busy collecting nuts from the large hazel tree they were hiding behind. It would tap the nut, examine it and then put it in one of two piles. Rosie was fascinated by this and could have watched the grey squirrel for hours. She knew one thing though, the calmness at this point was about to change. Ben had gotten good at judging the wind and the ground so he could sneak up unawares on some small animals. Being just under 6 inches tall helped too, he supposed being smaller than the squirrel meant the squirrel didn't see him as a threat. Ben snuck up to within grabbing distance, grabbed two handfuls of fur and held on for dear life. The squirrel didn't move; it froze and fixed a mesmerised stare into the distance. It was twitching ever so slightly like it had heard a noise or was stunned. Ben was just about to claim success to Rosie when the squirrel bolted up the tree and into the branches. It darted from branch to branch almost in circles, so fast it was nearly a blur. Ben could feel his lunch about to rise from his stomach; the sheer speed of the squirrel was unbelievable. He couldn't even make out the scenery as it flew past him or where Rosie was. The squirrel then darted down the hazel tree, at which point Ben let go. He couldn't stand any more of the jostling around, and the bile making its way into his throat was enough. He hit the ground with a thud rolling to a stop a few feet from Rosie, who was in hysterics.

"Your eyes were popping out of your head Ben," she said, "Your face was a picture. It was like that time we caught Tom and Jillian having sex!!" she continued to laugh.

Ben sat up and looked at the squirrel in the distance. The world was still turning in his vision, and he had to shake his head a few times to clear it. Once his vision had settled, he could see the squirrel was still standing there looking at him, head slightly cocked to one side. Ben could have sworn the squirrel was laughing too if squirrels could laugh. It was almost mocking him as it stared at him, like a little statue. Ben was still trying to get his bearings when he heard a voice in the distance.

"Ben, Rosie, time to come home now, the night is drawing in," the voice said. It was their mother calling them to come home.

Ben got up and walked over to Rosie, who was bent over, still laughing. He punched her lightly on the shoulder to which she flinched but continued to laugh.

"Well, I guess I can cross that one of my bucket list then," he said with a sigh.

"Me too," she replied.

"You didn't ride" he exclaimed

"No, but I got to see you make an absolute fool of yourself," she sniggered.

They both started walking towards their mother's voice through the tall grass and the weeds. The sun, setting in the distance, created shadows from the foliage, they were getting longer as it dipped out of sight. Being so small had its advantages, but it also meant it took ages to get anywhere, hence trying to tame the squirrel. Ben believed it was the group's next form of transport. As they walked, the dandelions began to tower over their heads along with the grass and the brush. The dandelions looked like tall thin soldiers with yellow hats guarding the pathway home. It was like a rainforest here; huge plants were everywhere, and the grass was so thick it was difficult to part. This wilderness had many dangers, but the biggest predator they faced by far were the foxes and badgers, not tigers and leopards. They didn't talk much on the way back. They never did, the days always seemed the same, so there was not much to talk about really. Yes, Rosie annoyed the hell out of Ben and vice versa, but neither of them left each other on their own, it was far too dangerous. They looked out for one another even if they wouldn't admit it.

They arrived at a clearing surrounded by hawthorn bushes and made their way through the small opening they had exited out of this morning. The area had several tents set up in it, just like scout huts. It almost looked like a jamboree or cub scout meeting with the large campfire in the middle. Left of the campfire was a woman in her late forties working around some pots and a cooking stove. Ben and Rosie could smell the food she was cooking; both of their stomachs began to gurgle and groan.

"Hi, mom," they both said in unison.

"Hey, guys, did you get up to much today?" she said

Rachel was also super fit and stunning with long dark hair and features reminiscent of Phoebe Cates. Rosie was the image of her, but with fewer experience lines on her face.

"Ben tried to ride a squirrel," Rosie blurted out.

"Shh, Rosie," whispered Ben.

"What have I told you about getting near the wildlife," Rachel said, standing up.

"Umm, not to?" he replied, almost like a question.

"Now, now, he's not hurt, and I'm sure he won't be doing it again" a gruff voice came from one of the tents. It was their father, Cameron.

Dr Cameron was a physicist and astrologer. He too was well built like an Olympian with short greying hair and a greying goatee. Cameron was taller than the rest of them by a quarter-inch, and he was undoubtedly the man of the family. Cameron was old fashioned but respectful to his wife and kids, treating them like any model father and husband would. He had also benefitted from the years of no smoking, no alcohol, and no fast food. Out here, they lived off the land and caught what they ate. Fresh water was caught in rain traps and boiled on the fire. They had no toxins, chemicals, or disease to contend with, it was almost the best way to live, except for the lack of other people.

Cameron had received a letter thirty years ago, offering him the opportunity to travel into space in an experimental craft and seek new life and new planets. It sounded like the start of an episode of Star Trek:

"Space, the final frontier
These are the voyages of the Starship Enterprise
Its five-year mission
To explore strange new worlds
To seek out new life
And new civilisations
To boldly go where no man has gone before."

Cameron couldn't pass up an opportunity like that and to top it off they wanted his fiancée to come along too. Neither of them had any ties and opportunities like that doesn't come along every day, so they went for it. That's when they met the colleagues that they live with today.

"It's not the point, they know how dangerous it is out there," Rachel said.

"Let's just sit down and talk about it," he said soothingly touching his wife on the shoulder.

They all took a chair around the fire while Rachel served up the food she had been cooking. She had been cooking vegetable soup from the garden they had planted earlier in the year. They managed to find several edible plants and the seeds they had brought with them had helped tremendously. Being only six inches tall, one carrot fed them for up to a week, but growing them was an enormous task.

They ate their soup and discussed the events of the day; the squirrel incident was skipped over with a "Don't do it again," and they got on to the subject of how they ended up where they are. It was Ben and Rosie's favourite subject; they would learn all about their parent's childhood and where they came from, how they had never met anyone else like them, and where everybody else was. Cameron would talk about spaceships, shrinking machines and science labs. He would talk about all the people they once knew, and he would talk about how big they used to be before they ended up here.

"Dad, please tell us the story again, please," begged Rosie

"Ok then, I will," he replied.

The story was always the same plot, but he would always add something interesting to it they had never heard before.

CHAPTER 2 – THE EXPEDITION OF ALL EXPEDITIONS

Thursday, June 26 – 1980

The group exited the elevator into a corridor that stretched out as far as the eye could see. There were no windows, and fresh air came in through vents in the ceiling. Light emitted from the floor giving the corridor a futuristic feel. They must have been at least three or four floors underground at this point. It felt like a nuclear bunker, like the ones shown in some war films. It was quiet except for their footsteps and the grey walls screaming what a dull colour they were. The corridor was a very clinical and sterile environment with no-nonsense signage on the doors they passed, Room 8, Room 9, bathroom, and so on. They reached Room 16, and the Corporal at the front stopped and turned on his heels.

"Inside please," the soldier asked and opened the door stiffly.

In the room was a long table with seven chairs around it, three either side and one at the head of the table. Sat in the head chair was a large balding man, sat upright and stiff, and showing no expression at all. The rest of the room was mostly bare except for a table to the right. On the table were jugs of water and glasses. There was a large TV screen on the wall above the man in the chair, currently blank like a window to nothing. The room was a dull grey in colour, giving it a military feel.

The man in the chair stood up, saluted to the Corporal, and addressed the group.

"Good evening, I am General Hastings. I trust you had a pleasant journey?" he asked, "Please take a seat."

They all took seats around the table, and the Corporal brought over the jugs of water and glasses. He set them down in the middle of the table and stood to attention next to the door.

"That will be all Corporal," the General said.
The Corporal turned and saluted the General who, in turn, saluted back. Then the Corporal turned around swiftly and headed out the door and closing it behind him.

"So, let's get acquainted," said the General sitting down.
He produced six ID badges and began handing them out, saying their names in turn before handing it to them.

"Dr Cameron Hill, Dr Rachel Hill, Captain David Beckett, Colonel Julia Hoffman, Dr Jillian Peach, Major Thomas Reid, Private Doug Balaski, and Dr Peter Miles," he said this with a slight smile on his face.

"I take it you've all got to know each a little bit on the journey here," the General continued.

They all looked at one another and nodded somewhat unenthusiastically. The General proceeded to introduce each of them in turn with their credentials and their ranks or experience.

"Dr Cameron Hill is a Physicist and expert in astrology. His wife, Dr Rachel Hill, is also a scientist specialising in undiscovered plants and animals. Colonel Julia Hoffman is a highly decorated Naval officer, and Major Thomas Reid is a highly decorated Sergeant Major in the army. Dr Jillian Peach is a medical doctor and experienced field medic. Private First-class Doug Balaski is also a highly decorated soldier. Dr Peter Miles is a Psychotherapist with top recommendations from the white house and the president himself."

The General sat back in his chair and sipped at a glass of water. He looked around the room at the perplexed faces of his colleagues at the table.

"Well, its time I brought you up to speed," the General continued.

"General, what are we doing here?" asked Dr Hill.

"Please, let me explain, and I'll answer all your questions afterwards" he replied and began to explain the situation.

"America's race to put a man on the moon was very much successful. The landing on the moon was real, and Neil Armstrong and Buzz Aldren walking on the moon was real. All the hoax theories are false. What isn't true is the length of time it took them to reach the moon, it wasn't three days. What the public was not told was the fact the journey took three years, and the launch of Apollo 11 did not carry Aldren and Armstrong, but they did go up in Apollo 4. The reason that this was covered up was that they were unsure if they would even make it. A week before the landing of the alleged Apollo 11, they realised Apollo 4 would make it to the moon and successfully land. Apollo 11 was a remotely controlled craft that is probably still orbiting the earth to this day. So, they edited the footage. What was aired was pre-recorded a couple of days before the event as we know it."

Several of the team gasped at this and went to ask some questions, but General Hastings put a hand up and continued.

"What we have been working on is a faster way to travel in space so that we can explore further afield. Before anyone asks, we have not invented any warp engines or teleportation. It's not Star Trek. What we have found, with the help of modern technology, is a quicker, safer way to travel light years into space in exponentially shorter time scales. We have developed a craft that will, theoretically, go from earth to the moon in less than a day. It is top-secret technology, that information cannot leave this room; you've all signed the confidentiality agreement. So if you look to the screen, you'll see the plans for the craft in question. You can see the ship will house six people comfortably, with separate sleeping quarters, labs, mess halls, and armoires. There is a flight deck at the front near the top of the craft. It has state of the art viewing screens and shielding. The plan is for this ship to be able to sustain the crew for multiple years so that they can achieve deep space exploration comfortably without any danger."

On the screen was what could only be described as a space-ship straight out of Star Wars. It looked like it was equipped with weapons or laser cannons. The ship was silver in colour and resembled an oversized Boeing aeroplane minus the wings and tail section. Cargo doors were at the rear, and you could see the bridge at the front of the craft.

"I think this is a good point for some questions, don't you?" said the General.

"General, Looking at these schematics, this ship" he mimed quotations with his fingers "must be massive, where in the world could something of this scale be built, not here at Goonhilly that's for sure" Cameron sounded very sarcastic at this point.

"Doctor, I can assure you that this craft is genuine and 90% complete, with final works to be completed as we speak," the General replied.

"General, whereabouts is this craft," asked Dr Miles

"It's right here," the General replied.

The table fell silent as they all knew Goonhilly earth station is just a communications array, not a space station.

"The next part of this presentation will help you understand how this all works," said the General, motioning them all to calm down.

The ship itself measures just twelve meters in length, its currently in the hanger adjacent to Arthur.

Arthur was the world's first open parabolic antenna and is on the Goonhilly earth station near Helston in Cornwall.

At this point, General Hastings new he was losing the team; they started to talk amongst themselves and snigger at each other. He reached down to the table and picked up a radio.

"Send in Dr Strauss please," he said into the radio.

"Yes, Sir," came the reply from the radio through the static.

The door to the room opened, and the Corporal from earlier came in and walked up to the table. He placed what looked like an action figure on the table, saluted the General, turned on his heels and left the room, closing the door behind him. The team looked at each other confused. They began to smile and frown at what was on the table in front of them.

"Excuse me, ladies and gentlemen," said a voice with a thick German accent

They all looked to the action figure standing on the table and then at one another. Dr Jillian Peach began to panic. You could see the alarm in her face; if she was trying to hide it, she was doing a terrible job of it.

"W, w, what the hell is that" exclaimed Julia Hoffman, pointing at the table.

"Please calm yourselves. I am Dr Herman Strauss from Hamburg Germany" he announced, "As you can see, I am currently a 1/12th my normal size, and I can assure I am quite, quite well. It is a pleasure to meet you all," he continued.

"General, what was in that water?" asked Cameron

"This is all for real Doctor" replied the General

"Oh, my god," said Jillian and started to breathe erratically

"Please calm yourself," the General said, "Please listen to Dr Strauss. We're all scientists here."

"Yes, allow me to explain," said the tiny doctor.

In the early 1960s, we successfully managed to reduce the size of several inanimate objects, vehicles, and other stationary equipment. We then moved onto animal testing, and with some regrettable accidents. We perfected the process and managed to successfully reduce a human to one-twelfth of his original size, namely myself. Since we achieved this, we have been working closely with the British and American armies to find a way to travel in space faster and more efficiently. What we have found is that a conventional craft is far too big, and it takes a lot of energy to pass through the earth's atmosphere, thus burning up most of its fuel before it has even left the planet. With the smaller craft, it can pass through the atmosphere with ease and navigate space more effectively. The reduction in weight makes a significant difference to the velocity of the ship as well. We predict, with the fuel-saving alone, we can travel that much faster on the fuel we have saved.

"Surely there's no resistance when travelling through

space," asked Rachel "What difference would it make how big the craft is"

"Unfortunately, that is the current misconception. Reality is that manoeuvring through space as we know it has an adverse effect on any spacecraft. The smaller the craft, the less resistance." replied Dr Strauss.

"I think we need to see this craft to believe this," said Cameron

"Agreed, please follow me" the General got up from his chair and headed for the door. He opened the door and stepped out.

"General, do you mind?" asked Dr Strauss

"Of course, Corporal, please assist Dr Strauss."

"Yes, Sir"

The Corporal entered the room and picked up Dr Strauss in both hands. They followed General Hastings along the same drab grey corridor passing the rooms in descending order until they arrived at the elevator they came down in this morning. They entered the elevator, and the doors closed slowly in front of them with a slight squeak. They were in silence as they rose in the elevator to ground level. Everyone was in deep thought about what they had seen and what they were about to see. Suddenly a high-pitched squeak came from in the lift followed by a slightly pungent odour. They all looked at each other accusingly before they all burst out laughing, except the General who was stood stoically at the back of the elevator.

"Apologies, lifts make me nervous," said Dr Strauss from the palm of the Corporal's hand.

It reminded Cameron of Peter Sellers in Revenge of the Pink Panther. The elevator came to a stop, and the doors opened to the foyer of the main reception. They made their way to the main entrance doors. They were glass with metal frames. You could see the sunlight and blue skies outside of the doors, which was a welcome sight after being underground all morning. The General opened the doors and stepped into the sunlight, feeling the warmth straight away. The team gathered behind the General, and the Corporal moved alongside him, holding Dr Strauss.

"I need to give you the opportunity to back out now if you feel the need to," the General stated with his back to them.

"Are you kidding? This is unbelievable," said Cameron, his wife Rachel nodding in agreement.

"Agreed, I can't miss this, I knew we were going to be working on a space program, but when I found out it was here, I assumed it was just communications, I'm in," said Major Thomas Reid.

The others all agreed that they wanted to see this spaceship. None of them wanted to leave and regret not doing this for the rest of their lives.

"Good, then let's move on," said the General and one by one they filed in behind him as he moved along the pathway, the Corporal and Dr Strauss bringing up the rear.

CHAPTER 3 – THE TEAM

Thursday, August 12^{th,} 2010

"I hear you've been bothering the wildlife again, Ben," Said Major Thomas Reid walking up to the campfire.
Ben looked up, sheepishly and grinned.

"We'll need to call you 'squirrel wrangler' from now on," Said Tom with a smirk.

He took a seat and rested his rifle against his chair. Thomas, or Tom as he preferred, was a military man through and through, he bled camo. He was the protector of the group, which was a full-time job, especially when the Hill kids went exploring. Tom was a very muscular built man with short-cropped hair and was clean-shaven, ish. If he stood still long enough, he did look like a G.I. Joe or maybe an action man figure. All he'd ever known was the army, from childhood he was an army brat and followed his parents wherever they got stationed. He was just twenty at the start of this, and now he was fifty, but you wouldn't know it, like the others, the healthy diet and exercise had kept him young. They had been in the wilds for thirty years now, and with him, they wouldn't have lasted ten years. He was responsible for taking out the hungry fox of 1980 and the curious rat of June 2000. Since Ben and Rosie had come along, he had mellowed a lot, and they treated him as an uncle, and he treated them as a nephew and niece.

Tom had served multiple tours and won several medals for his service. He was a very decorated soldier by the time he was twenty but had always dreamed of going into space. That dream almost came true when a letter arrived in the post giving him the opportunity to go on a mission to the moon. Best of all, it was in the UK. Having no family to miss, he jumped at the opportunity and signed on. He had made his way to Helston in Cornwall the next day and arrived at Goonhilly earth station the day after. That's where he met Rachel and Cameron Hill, Captain David Beckett, and Dr Jillian Hoffman. That's also where things took a turn for the worst, and they lost Peter and Doug.

"So, what's cooking then," Tom asked

"The usual" replied Rachel

"Nice, it doesn't get old," he said smiling

"Your delightful Tom," she stated blushing

"Dad is telling the story again," Ben said with a mouthful

"Don't tell me I'm missing the story," a female voice said from another tent "Wait for me" it was Jillian.

Jillian was a medical doctor and field medic, gaining her doctorate at twenty. She was one of the youngest to do so. Jillian had long flowing red hair, a very athletic frame, and a face covered in freckles. With the lack of suntan lotion, she often spent her day in the tents or covered up with hats and jackets. With her fair milky skin, she always burned severely, and out here in the wilds, there was no treatment available. They had managed to keep the supplies going, but they also managed to derive penicillin from some moulds they had found. Being a keen botanist as well as doctor, Jillian had managed to cook up all sorts of medicines. Jillian was invited to join the crew as she too was an only child with no other living family. She was also young enough to last the multiple-year mission.

"Where are we up to then?" Tom asked

"They, sorry, you're going to see the ship," Rosie said, grinning.

"Where's David?" asked Cameron

"I'm in here, I'm not in the mood for 'the story' tonight, you guys carry-on," said Captain Beckett

David Beckett was a first-class pilot, top of his class in all his training, and he had multiple hours in multiple aircraft. He also had qualifications in diving and submersibles and was a real petrol head. David loved his American cars or yank tanks as Tom called them. He had a 1971 Camaro in navy blue. It was his reason for getting out of bed in the morning. He often wondered what happened to it as he hasn't seen it in so long, "It's probably rotted away by now" he often thought to himself. The years had made him quite cynical and very, very miserable, he was into his fifties, and he had significant plans that never happened. He wanted to get married, have kids, and travel, but that bastard letter had to come and tempt him. The letter offered him the chance to fly a prototype spacecraft, who would pass that up, so he went along. He was now stuck with the Hill family, Tom and Jillian, who had obviously paired up, and then there was Julia. He had a massive crush on Julia, but she had no interest in him, or so she said, he could never tell. She was never around anyway, always wandering about looking at trees and flowers, he had the feeling she may be losing her marbles.

Julia was a bit of a free spirit. She never used to be. Julia was David's number two, and boy was she in charge when he wasn't around. In the last twenty-five years, Julia had drifted into madness due to being lost, and due to the isolation. Julia had now made it back to reality, starting with the birth of Benjamin and getting better from there. She still wondered off now and again, but it was her way of dealing with the isolation. Julia was an approximate 5ft 10, average build, blond hair, and a fair bosom, which David had a job to look away from when Julia was around. She wasn't as striking as Jillian, but she was far from ugly. Cameron believed being stuck out here in the wilds had worked a few screws loose in her head, and Julia was dealing with it in her way. Rachel and Cameron knew where she was tonight; she was in her tent sleeping. Julia would probably awake in the night and wander off for a few hours as she usually did. Julia did always came back.

"So, we were following General Hastings across Goonhilly Earth Station," said Cameron.

CHAPTER 4 – GOONHILLY

Thursday, June 26 – 1980

Following General Hastings, they could see the giant satellite dishes around them, and in front was 'Arthur.' 'Arthur' was a vast, imposing sight to behold. It looks big from the road, but being up close to it puts it in perspective. It was tremendous, to say the least, it is 85 feet in diameter and weighs in at a whopping 1118 tonnes. Looking around the site, you could see soldiers posted at all access points to the site, and they were armed as well. There were multiple army vehicles parked to the right in the visitor's car park and soldiers patrolling the grounds, saluting the General as they passed. Goonhilly was known as a communications centre but who would have thought it would be a spaceport.

The other sixty-plus satellite dishes were glinting in the sunshine, shining like mirrored discs reflecting the suns rays across the lands. It was so bright you could see them for miles around. The area surrounding the site was very green and flat with the odd clump of trees and gorse brush. The nearest town was several miles away. As they passed by Arthur, they could see the hanger that General Hastings was describing earlier. It wasn't impressive by any means, your average warehouse-type building. It blended in well with the rest of the complex, not standing out. You wouldn't give the building a second glance if you didn't know what was in it. As they approached the entrance, you could see the soldier's inside standing guard through the lightly frosted glass doors. As General Hastings approached the glass door, one of the soldiers stepped forward and opened it like a hotel concierge. Both soldiers saluted as they entered the building and closed the doors behind them.

In front of them stood a sealed metal door, like a bank vault, with a massive wheel on the front. The General stepped up to a small control panel to the right of the door. He looked into a small aperture above it, and within a few moments, they could hear clicks and clunks, and the wheel started to turn. The door slowly began to open with a slight hiss like an airlock, revealing its considerable thickness. One by one, they all stepped through the door and were greeted by several technicians in lab coats who handed them anti-static overshoes, safety glasses and lab coats. They were each relieved of their personal belongings, which were put in trays marked with their names and then shelved. They were then led through a plastic curtain into another dull grey corridor with three doors on the right side and one on the left. As they walked along the hall, the doors on the right read 'Reduction Room', 'Navigation,' and 'Briefing Room'. On the left were large double doors labelled 'Hanger.' General Hastings opened both swing doors to the Hanger and beckoned to them to walk through.

Inside the hanger were various workstations and machinery, and in the centre was a large metal structure with what looked like a giant Star Wars toy spaceship on it. Walking up to the ship was quite surreal, and it was astounding to see something so impressive on such a small scale. Technicians in lab coats were meticulously working on the vessel with robotic arms and huge magnifiers. On the supporting structure were several six-inch-high technicians. They were coming in and out of the hull of the ship with tools and equipment. One of the normal-sized Technicians stepped forward and greeted them all with a handshake and a smile.

"Welcome everyone, my name is Dr Ian Jinx, and I am the lead technician under Dr Strauss. I assume you have Dr Strauss with you?" said Ian looking through the group of people.

"I'm here, Ian," came a small voice from the Corporal's hands.

The Corporal stepped forward, let Dr Strauss walk onto the

supporting structure holding the Ship. He then turned, saluted, and marched off to the entrance to the hanger. Dr Strauss made his way up to a small podium by the ship. Dr Jink moved a large mobile TV screen into position adjacent to the vessel and stepped back to join the team.

Ian was a slight man with a balding head and a noticeable bend in his back, giving him a sort of hunchback appearance, a bit like Igor, Doctor Frankenstein's assistant.

"Ladies and Gentlemen, I present to you the Goon Mk 1. We have built this state-of-the-art vessel right here at the Earth station. Built using the same reduction technology we developed in Germany. We build the parts and then reduce them in size in the reduction room; we then fit them to the ship. The ship measures 12.4 metres in length and 6.2 metres wide. She is also 5.8 meters high. It roughly equates to the size of a small cruise ship boat but reduced to ten percent of its original size." Dr Strauss explained

As Dr Strauss explained this, pictures were shown on the screen of the American Queen cruise ship to give some perspective. Photos of the Goon were displayed to show comparison next to the cruise ship and people. The group was noticeably in awe of this, and so far, no one had interrupted Dr Strauss, which surprised him a little. He clicked the remote and brought up a schematic of the inside of the ship. The schematic showed six decks onboard the vessel. The top floor was the bridge and navigation area. The second deck was living quarters with six separate units containing a living room, bedroom, bathroom, and kitchen dining area. There was also a communal living area with kitchen and entertainment areas with TVs, pool tables, etc. On the third deck were labs and medical suites with recovery rooms and clean rooms. On the fourth deck was what look to be storerooms and a biosphere with plants and vegetation inside. On the fifth deck was an armoury, and what seemed to be cells and shooting ranges. On the final sixth deck were storage and mechanical maintenance workshops for vehicles. The image showed two army spec land rovers and three enduro-style motorbikes. There were also two rib type boats on trailers and one large APC. In the middle of the craft was an elevator that accessed all the floors.

"So, do we have any questions?" asked Dr Strauss.

"Well, my first question is, what is it powered by, what engines does it have?" asked Major Reid.

"It has four prototype nuclear reactors that produce enough power and thrust to break free of the atmosphere and travel into space. It also has solar-powered engines that will move it through space with ease, charging with the sun's rays and captured by solar sails when deployed. Nuclear engines will only be for entering and exiting the atmospheres of planets." he replied.

"OK," Tom said quizzically.

"How long could we survive in the ship for?" asked Rachel

"There will be enough engine power for ten exits and re-entries, and solar power is nearly infinite. You will be provided with enough food and water to last ten years if needed. The Biosphere will also provide fresh fruit and vegetables for as long as it's looked after" replied Dr Strauss.

"That's a long time in space," said Peter

"You have the opportunity to take anything you wish for entertainment, within reason," replied the General, with a very slight smirk.

"What is our mission? It's beginning to sound like the plot from Star Trek," said Cameron.

"Your mission is to get the moon and back in record time," replied the General "If successful, we will then venture further afield. We will be briefing you on the mission in the morning. The first task is to reduce you all," said the General, Stoic as ever.

There looked at each other nervously, did they want to do this, what were the risks involved. There was plenty of evidence that it was a safe procedure, but being reduced to ten percent of your original size was a big step. They all wanted to go into space, and this may be their only chance. Besides, they had all signed the waivers before the meeting, so there was no turning back now. It was a chance in a lifetime.

"It's time we started the process, Dr Strauss," said, General

Hastings
"I believe so," he replied.

PART 2

CHAPTER 5 – A REDUCTION IN LIFE

Thursday, June 26 – 1980

They stood in a group behind General Hastings in anticipation of entering the 'Reduction Room'. The General had paused for a moment at the door, taking a moment to gather himself before entering. He had witnessed many reductions over the last few years, some of which had not gone to plan. The General always paused before entering the room, the memories of the failed reductions prodding at his mind making him hesitate. He let out a deep breath and opened the door, walking in as he did. The others filed in behind, forming a semi-circle by the big machine in the centre of the room.

It was a deceivingly large room for the single door in the hallway, with no windows and light emitting from the floor and the ceiling. There was a red glow to the lighting which made the room look futuristic and almost fake. The machine in the centre of the room wasn't that impressive. It was very clinical and straightforward. It comprised of a booth or chamber with a frosted glass door and what looked like an engine behind it. The booth was like a hotel shower cubical with stainless steel walls and floors. It seemed very medical in design, with ninety percent of it made out of stainless steel. The rest of the room was bare apart from a larger cubical to the rear, with glass windows facing the machine. There were lockers to the right of the room, dull in design and the same colours as the room.

"This is the Reduction machine," announced General Hastings.

"We will begin shrinking each one of you, in turn, starting with you Dr Hill," he said pointing at Cameron

"The process will take approximately five minutes to complete. Once complete, you will be asleep for at least ten hours to help you adjust to your new stature," the General continued.

"You will need to be naked during the procedure as your clothes will not shrink with you. New clothes have been made for all of you and are in the lockers to the right."

"I guess I best prepare myself then," said Cameron looking noticeably nervous.

"Please can the rest of you follow me into the viewing room, Dr Hill, please remove your clothes and step into the cubicle," the General asked.

Rachel rushed up to Cameron and planted a kiss on his lips. She pulled him in close to hug him tightly.

"Are we sure about this" she whispered in his ear

"I think we're past the point of no return, my love," he replied, glancing over at the General.

Dr Strauss and Dr Jinx had made their way into the viewing room and were checking the machine's controls. Dr Strauss was up on a platform or table so he could see out the glass. The rest of the group made their way into the room, talking amongst each other as they entered. Cameron and Rachel were still holding each other as the General approached them.

"It's time Cameron," he said

Rachel let him go and headed for the viewing room, turning at the door and mouthing the words 'I love you' before entering the room. The General then followed and closed the door behind him. Cameron got undressed and piled his clothes to one side of the chamber. He couldn't decide what was worse, being naked in front of everyone or the thought of being shrunk. Looking down, Cameron realised one part of him was already shrinking, that maybe the cold or perhaps the fear of what was about to happen. He instinctively put both hands in front of his manhood and blushed.

"Please enter the cubicle, Dr Hill," a voice said from an unseen speaker in the room.

Cameron opened the door and stepped inside, flinching at the coldness of the stainless-steel floor. He turned to face the entrance and closed the door in front of him. His breathing was fast and short fogging up the already lightly frosted glass.

"Please stand still while we complete the procedure. We will begin in 3, 2, 1" the same almost robotic voice said out of the speakers.

There was a glow of red light inside the cubicle, which got brighter and brighter; the others had to shield their eyes from it. Cameron closed his eyes tightly and cupped his package, instinctively protecting it for some unknown reason. The machine began to hum loudly and vibrate softly under his feet. The thrum of the engine was making him feel sleepy. He started to drift away in his mind, the sounds disappearing, and the vibrating fading away.

The machine stopped humming, and the light inside dimmed and faded out. Ian Jinx walked to the viewing room door, opened it, and walked out into the reduction room towards the machine. He stopped at the lockers and retrieved what looked like an open tote toolbox with rows of small seats in it. Ian also took out a set of little clothing in the form of a pair of jeans and a plain black polo shirt. He grabbed some tiny trainers and a blanket. Ian Walked over to the machine, placed the toolbox to one side, and opened the door. He reached inside and picked up what looked like a naked action man, but a lot more detailed. Ian took the small blanket and wrapped the now reduced version of Cameron in it. He sat him in the toolbox and strapped him into one of the seats. Cameron looked slumped in the seat, but Dr Hill gave a thumbs up to the viewing window.

"Dr Hill is fine. I assure you; he will wake up tomorrow feeling like a new man, literally," Dr Strauss assured everyone in the room. "Dr Hill, it is your turn, my dear," he said to Rachel.

Rachel stepped nervously through the open viewing room door and headed over to Dr Jinx. She looked in the open toolbox carrier and could see Cameron sitting there, obviously fast asleep.

She saw his now tiny chest moving up and down, showing that he was breathing normally and sighed with relief. Dr Jinx moved the carrier over to the lockers and nodded at Rachel. She moved up to the front of the machine and stood looking at the glass door on the cubicle. A little nervously, Rachel began to take off her clothes and stood in her underwear and paused. She, too, was unsure if being naked was the problem or the procedure. Rachel opened the door and then removed her bra and slowly slipped down her panties, adding them to her pile of clothes on the floor. Now she felt extremely conscious of her body. She could feel how hard her nipples were and saw they were poking out like bullets. Her hands were trying to cover the small triangular patch of pubic hair between her legs, trying to keep some dignity. She looked up at the viewing window. Her colleagues were all looking down at the floor out of respect. Dr Strauss was looking right at her, staring. Presumably because of the procedure and not her tight naked form, standing in front of him. If he were enjoying this, she would never know as he was so small and too far away to show any signs of arousal. It was so cold she began to shiver, her breasts quivering as she did and her whole body breaking out in goosebumps. She stepped into the cubicle, closed the door behind her, and closed her eyes.

"Please keep your eyes closed and stand a still as possible, Dr. hill. 3, 2, 1" the voice crackled over the speaker.

CHAPTER 6 – IT'S A BIG WORLD AFTER ALL

Friday, June 27^{th,} 1980

Cameron awoke in a medical suite, connected to multiple machines via his arms and chest. He was on a hospital-type bed with bright white sheets and soft pillows. Cameron couldn't remember being in a hospital and for the life of him, couldn't remember why he was there. Cameron looked up at the bright fluorescent lights on the ceiling, hoping to spark some memory of recent events. He looked around the room and could see five other beds in a row next to his, right next to him was his wife Rachel asleep. He looked across to the others in the beds and recognised them, he was struggling to remember who they were, but he knew them. Dr Strauss came into the room and walked up to Cameron with a smile on his face.

"Dr Hill, how are you feeling?" he asked

"Dr Strauss? I am having trouble remembering why I'm here" Cameron Replied

"That's perfectly normal. It will subside," Dr Strauss replied.

Cameron started to remember the procedure and the reduction process. He remembered being in the machine, he remembered the bright red light, and he remembered the nakedness.

"I take it the procedure wasn't a success?" Cameron asked.

"What makes you say that, Dr Hill?" he replied.

"Well, I'm not small, am I. The room is normal, and so am I,"

Cameron said.

"I think you misunderstand Dr Hill, why don't you take a look out the window," Dr Strauss replied.

Cameron swung his legs off the bed and stood up, shaky at first, but soon found his feet and walked to the window. He noticed the window was strange, the glass was at least a foot thick, and it was round in shape. Leaning up to the glass, Cameron looked outside. He was astonished at what he saw, giant people walking around an enormous aircraft hangar.

"We are in the Goon Mk1, Dr Hill. The procedure was a success for all of you," Dr Strauss said from across the room.

A hand reached into Cameron's and squeezed it tightly. It was Rachel stood next to him looking out the window. He put an arm around her and held her firmly, planting a kiss on her head. The others had risen from their beds and filed in around them. They were all now looking out the ship's portholes.

"Your new clothes are at the end of your beds, please get dressed and then make your way to the bridge on level 1. The elevator is located at the end of the corridor." Dr Strauss announced.

They all entered then lift together, Jillian pressed the button for the first floor, and the lift began to rise. Cameron was remembering the events leading up to the procedure and remembering the procedure itself. He remembered their last trip in an elevator together, and then he remembered Dr Strauss and let out a snigger. Rachel looked at him with a quizzical look on her face and a frown.

"What?" she asked

"I just remembered the last time we were in a lift. I remembered Dr Strauss and him letting one go," Cameron replied, laughing.

They all began to laugh out loud. It was a welcome feeling after waking up shrunk and disorientated.

The doors swished open on level one to an ample open space with several captain's type chairs facing an extra-large viewing port. Dr Strauss was standing next to the viewing port working on one of many control panels. He had his back to them as they entered the bridge. It looked like an episode Star Trek. Cameron and couldn't help but compare it, it was uncanny.

"Ah, hello team," said Dr Strauss "Good you are here, General Hastings will be addressing us shortly."

"Is he reduced too?" asked Jillian

"No, no he will be on the viewing screen shortly," Dr Strauss replied.

The viewing port flicked and turned to an image of a meeting room with General Hastings sat at a table with several other army personnel. He looked severe as ever and was sitting stiffly in anticipation of the upcoming meeting.

"Can you hear us, Dr Strauss?" he said

"Yes sir, we can hear you?" Dr Strauss replied

"Good, I hope everyone has recovered from the reduction procedure. As you can see, the ship is nearing completion, and we will soon be prepping it for launch. I want to start by assigning you your missions and positions as part of the crew. Captain Beckett, you will be the captain of the ship; you are in charge of this mission. Colonel Julia Hoffman, you are to be second in command and Captain Beckett's number two. Major Thomas Reid, you will be Sargent at Arms and the ship's security officer, your job is to protect the crew. Private Doug Balaski, you will assist Major Reid. Dr Jillian Peach, you are the ship's physician and doctor. Dr Rachel Hill and Dr Cameron Hill, you are the science team for the mission. Dr Peter Miles, you will be working closely with Dr Hill. You have all excelled in your fields and are our best hope to complete this mission" the General said.

He cleared his throat and took a sip of water.

"I'm afraid not all of this will be smooth sailing. We have had some push backs from higher up, and they are looking to shut us down. We will be moving up the launch before this can happen. We have put a lot of work into this program, and we are not about to give up now. You are all reduced already, and that will have all been for nothing." the General explained.

"Why are they trying to stop this mission?" asked Captain Beckett

"The Government decided that the reduction of people for this mission is unethical and the Government wants to put a stop to it" he replied

The General stood up and walked around the table up to the camera filling the viewing screen,

"I'm not going to lie to you. The Government want to bury this project and wipe out any evidence it existed," the General said quietly to them. "We launch in three days."

The screen went back to a clear window, and the sound crackled off. Cameron looked at the others in the room and thought for a moment. The crew was silent, digesting what they had just learned.

"How about a tour of the ship Dr Strauss," Cameron asked

"Of course, if you would all like to follow me, I will show you your quarters and the rest of the ship," Dr Strauss replied.

He led them to the elevator and let them enter before pressing the button for the sixth-floor and closing the doors. They arrived in a large open space with several vehicles parked in it. There was a workbench and cabinets to the rear of the deck and storage to their right. They could see the large door that gave access to the room from the outside, presumably for offloading vehicles and equipment. They all surveyed the room before re-entering the elevator and travelling to the fifth floor.

On the fifth floor, they saw the armoury and the few secure rooms or cells would be a more appropriate description. They headed up to the fourth floor and exited the lift onto an ample open space lined with storerooms and the Biosphere. They looked through the doors of the Biosphere and could see the plants and trees that were inside. It was like another world inside, out of place on a ship like this. On the third floor was the medical suite with state of the art equipment and several hospital beds. They woke up here this morning but only now they could see the extent of what was available to them.

After seeing all the other decks, they arrived on the second floor, which housed the living quarters and suites. Dr Strauss showed them their prospective quarters and stood to face them.

"It has been a long day, and I am sure you could all do with a rest. We will reconvene at 06:00hrs on the bridge."

Dr Strauss bid them all well in turn and returned to the elevator. They all wished each other well and went into their quarters for the night. Cameron and Rachel were sharing a suite and decided to get some dinner as they were both starving. It had been a truly eventful day, and they were looking forward to getting to bed for some well-earned rest. The suite was spacious, made up of four rooms, a kitchen, bathroom, lounge area, and a bedroom. It was very dull inside, made up of ocean grey and military grey paintwork and some minimalistic artwork. Though futuristic, it was functional and had all the amenities they could need. There was plenty of clothing in the cupboards in the bedroom in their sizes. There was also a large stock of food in the kitchen. Rachel and Cameron were keen to discover more of the ship but decided to get some rest. They took off their shoes and clambered into bed, holding each other waiting for sleep to take them, which it eventually did.

CHAPTER 7 – ESCAPE

Saturday 28th June 1980

Six am came quicker than Cameron would have liked, he was quite happy cuddled up to his wife in the surprisingly comfy bed in their quarters. The 6 am alarm was broadcast over the ship's tannoy system, and all of the team were now awake and getting ready for the mornings briefing. They all made their way to the bridge to meet Dr Strauss, dispersing from the elevator one at a time. Dr Strauss was in the middle of the room waiting for them.

"General Hastings has decided to have the briefing in the briefing room in the main building. If you would all like to make your way to the cargo deck, we will exit the ship from there."

They all entered the elevator, including Dr Strauss, who pushed the button for the sixth deck. The door swooshed open, and they exited the lift, gathering at the cargo doors. The cargo doors started to open surprisingly quickly to show a large carrier on the workbench next to the Goon Mk1. The tray had multiple seats with belts and a storage area in the back end. The large handle on the top made it look like an open tote tool bag or tray, a bit like a plumber might use to carry his tools. Dr Strauss walked up to the open door on the carrier and gestured for everybody to file inside.

Once they were all safely strapped in, Dr Jinx picked up the carrying tray and strode carefully across the room to the entrance of the hanger. He crossed the grey hallway and opened the briefing room door, stepping inside. Dr Jinx placed the carrier on the large table in the centre of the room. He then headed over to the counter on the right. The team exited the carrier one by one and stood facing the chair at the head of the table. Dr Jinx brought over seven leather chairs that had been reduced and placed them in a semi-circle on the table. They all took a seat and began chatting amongst one another about the quarters and the ship. They were all getting excited about the mission and knew it was nearly time to launch. It was all starting to sink in, and they were going into space. The door to the briefing room opened, and General Hastings walked in. He walked around the table and took the seat at the head chair. Dr Jinx took one of the chairs next to the General and turned to face everyone.

"Dr Jinx, are we on schedule," said the General

"Yes sir, the ship is ready, and the launch system is ready" he replied

"Good, we are going for launch tomorrow at 8 am," said the General

"Sir, what about training on flying the ship," asked Captain Beckett

"It's mostly automated so that we can train you during the flight, Dr Strauss will be with you to assist," replied General Hastings.

"This seems very rushed," said Cameron "Shouldn't we have some test runs?"

"We need to get you on your mission before they shut us down, the government are pushing to close this project" Replied General Hastings "We don't know when they are likely to come knocking and shut us down. If they find you here, it won't be right for you. They will shut you away and make you disappear. I won't let that happen."

An alarm started sounding over the tannoy system, a warning alarm not a wake-up call like this morning. The door to the briefing room flew open and banged the wall hard making a mark in the plaster. A Soldier rushed in clumsily and addressed the General.

"Sir, we have government officials at the gate with MI6 and the army. They are coming in," the Soldier said.

"Shit, that's it. The government is here to clean house, we need to get them out of here," the General said, gesturing to the team.

"What's going to happen to us," said Rachel, the emotion showing on her face.

"No time, get in the carrier now," he said.

They all entered the carrier, strapping in and holding on as the General grabbed the handle. He then rushed out of the door, quicker than they all expected. The ride was a lot rougher than usual due to the urgency in which General Hastings was moving, Rachel felt her stomach starting to turn. Dr Strauss had not strapped himself in correctly and was teetering close to the side of the carrier. With a jolt, he fell out of his seat and over the edge of the carrier. Dr Strauss locked eyes with Rachel. They were filled with urgency as he disappeared from view. General Hastings didn't notice despite the calls and screams from them, and he just kept going. They burst out into the daylight from the hangar entrance and were moving fast to a nearby land rover. Dr Jinx came out of the hangar holding a large box. He was following closely behind, and you could see the worry in his face. General hasting opened the rear door of the land rover and strapped the carrier in the back. Dr Jinx placed the box at the end of the carrier and ran around to the passenger door. They heard a shot, and Dr Jinx fell to the floor, there was a splat of blood on the window, and the door was left flapping in the wind.

Rachel let out a scream of anguish, so Cameron held Rachel tightly to calm her. General Hasting got in the driver's side and started the land rover. He headed for the fence line, the passenger door slamming shut as they sped away. He was moving fast, not slowing down as the fence drew closer to them. The land rover burst through the perimeter fence with a crash sending metal sections over the roof and to the sides. The general wrestled the land rover and plummeted down the embankment into the brush surrounding the Earth station. A couple of shots rang off the rear of the landrover. One broke through the glass and striking the general in the left shoulder, and he let out a pained cry. He drove for a few more meters, stopping near some trees. The General jumped out of the driver's door getting caught up on the seat belt, but getting clear in a few seconds. He ran around to the back of the vehicle, threw open the door and grabbed the carrier. Unstrapping it and removing it from the back compartment of the landrover in one quick movement. He rushed over to the trees, placed the carrier next to a large oak and knelt to address them.

"Hide in the brush and trees and don't come out till I return. I will come back for you" the General said quietly

The General ran back to the Land Rover and drove away. He headed in the direction of the road bouncing over the embankments and on to the tarmac. Several black trucks came up behind him, passing him and blocking him in. One of the drivers got out, and calmly walked up to the landrover door, raising a gun to the window and pulling the trigger. The bang was startling, making them freeze and all fall silent. Though they could barely see the trucks in the distance, they knew that the General was gone. Major Tom quickly got everyone to move and follow him into the Brush to hide. He knew that the army would be looking for them soon.

PART 3

CHAPTER 8 – A DIFFERENT WORLD

Wednesday, September 3rd, 1980

A few weeks had passed since they were left in the wilds, not knowing exactly where they were. The brush was immense around them with Dandelions like small trees and grass taller than their heads. No one had come to look for them since the General dropped them off, so now they were trying to find their way back to the Earth Station. The box that Dr Jinx had put in the carrier had contained weapons, clothing, and food supplies. There were seeds, blankets, and tools for gardening. It looked like this was readily prepared for their journey into space. It was similar looking to the crates in the cargo hold on the Goon Mk1.

They had set up a camp under an oak tree near where General Hastings left them. Major Tom and Captain Beckett were taking turns in securing the site in the day and at night. As the days and nights drew on more and more animals were showing interest in them, and the only thing that would keep them away was the rifles from the supply box. There were also medicines with supplies, but nowhere near enough. They would have to ration them and only treat what essential or life-threatening. Water was the easy part, catching the rain and storing it in empty food containers and bottles gave them plenty to use.

After witnessing the death of General Hastings, they were all shaken up and what had happened to Dr Strauss, was he still alive or did he get captured. They needed to get back to Goonhilly somehow. They were so far away they couldn't see the station and had no idea which way to go. Major Tom suggested finding the road and following that back to the station, which they all agreed to.

"We need to start hunting and gathering food, that food won't last us," said Jillian

"I know, we need to think about foraging and maybe growing some food" replied Cameron

Tom and David were searching the area for signs of civilisation, roads, or buildings. Because they were lost in the wilderness, it was hard to decide which way to head. They had all lost their bearings during the escape. To someone six inches tall, the wilds were never-ending, even the grass was a nightmare to get through. There was all manner of plants, bushes, trees, shrubs, and animals out there. The insects were the comparative size of dogs or large cats. It was quite nerve-racking, being next to a beetle the size of an Alsatian. The insects weren't the problem, though. It was the rodents, badgers, and foxes that you had to watch out for. They were vicious and always hungry. These animals were looking for their next meal, and it seemed like humans smelled so good. So far, they were just curious, but their visits to their camp were getting more frequent, it was only a matter of time before something terrible would happen. Firing off the rifles in the animal's direction was enough to scare them away for now, but soon it will take more than that.

They decided to head west, or what they believed to be west according to the sun. They knew that they had headed east when they escaped. The going was tough through the undergrowth, especially with carrying the supplies they had. They decided to leave some of the provisions behind and return for them once they had set up another camp. They found a clearing about six hours into their journey. By this time, they were all exhausted and glad to find somewhere to stop and rest. Tom and Cameron began setting up camp with a little help from the others. They made three large tents from the supplies they had brought with them and constructed a large campfire in the centre of the clearing. Latrines were setup up approximately five minutes walk from the camp, the rest of the area was then swept for insects and animal burrows. Surrounding the camp were Cornish heath and black bog rush with purple moor grass and some conifer trees in the distance. They were well hidden and had fresh water nearby from a small stream feeding a pool in the rock.

Tom was out looking for firewood when he heard a rustling behind him. He turned quickly raising his rifle and pointing directly at Jillian. He promptly pointed it back at the ground, keeping his eyes on her. Jillian smiled and moved slowly towards him, the sun making her glow as seductively meandered over to him. She began to undress, letting her clothes fall to the floor one by one. Within a long minute, she was down to her underwear and within reach of Tom. Tom had to rub his eyes as he couldn't believe what he was seeing. This definitely aroused him, but it felt like a dream. Jilian put her hands on his and made him drop the rifle while pulling his hands onto her body. She had a fantastic body, and Tom knew this from when they had first met. He ran his hands up her thighs and waist onto her back. With one hand, he unsapped her bra, releasing her large natural breasts. By this time Jillian had unbuttoned his trousers and dropped them to the floor. The large member jutting out from his waist was hard to miss. Julia grabbed his penis and stroked it in her hand, making Tom quiver with excitement. Tom removed his clothes frantically and led down on the floor, letting Jillian straddle him like a cowgirl. Tom thrust himself into her, making her yelp with pleasure and go week at the knees. They made love like this for nearly half an hour climaxing together in a crescendo of screams and groans. Getting dressed Jillian whispered to him.

"Let's keep this a secret for now."

Tom nodded in agreement and followed her back to camp. He was watching her backside sway in front of him. Jillian knew he was watching and made sure it swayed seductively as she walked. Tom was feeling pretty high right now and planned to do this again when they could next disappear and get some alone time.

By nine pm, they settled around the campfire and cooked

some of the food they had brought with them. The soup was on the menu tonight with black herbal tea made by Dr Peach. It was a well-earned meal, and they were hungry from today's journey, especially since they had to set up camp as well. Tom was going to head back in the morning with David to collect the rest of the supplies and salvage what they could from the carrier. The night had set in now, and the skies were clear with numerous stars glinting above them. The temperature had dropped considerably in the last hour, and they were huddled together around the fire with blankets sipping tea. It was deathly quiet except for those sounds insects make during the night, crickets chirping and flies buzzing around.

"How long do you think it will take for us to find the earth station?" Rachel asked the group

"I have no idea. We don't even know where we are right now." Tom replied

"We need to find the road or any road for that matter" added David deep in thought

"Shhh, it's gone silent, no bug noises or any noises," said Tom

"What do you mean?" asked Jillian

"Look," said Tom point towards the edge of the camp.

On the edge of the camp above, some Cornish heath was a pair of sparkling eyes, flames from the fire flicking in them. They all froze. Steamy breath blew below the eyes in the darkness like smoke from the nostrils of a dragon. Tom reached across for his rifle and picked it up by the butt end, cocking it slowly as he brought it to his lap. David did the same getting ready to aim at the unseen beast in the darkness.

"Stay by the fire" whispered Tom to the others

A snout started to come into view over the bushes black around the nostrils with scarlet red fur running back towards the eyes. Then slowly, the animal's whole head came into view. It was a fox, a male, large and intimidating easing its way through the brush into the clearing. It was cautious of the fire but intrigued enough to come in and sniff around. Rachel let out a yelp of fear, which attracted the attention of the fox and it bared its teeth and began growling. The fox snapped at Doug Balaski grabbing him by the arm and dragging him towards the bushes, Doug was screaming as the fox pulled him away.

"Oh my god, help him," screamed Jillian.

Tom and David open fire on the fox, hitting shot after shot at the fox's head and side, this angered and hurt the fox, but it still dragged Doug away into the darkness. They could hear Doug's scream muted in the distance until a sickening crunch came out of the night, and the screams stopped.

They were all in shock; they were unprepared for this and never thought that a fox would be the one to get them. The night was silent again, and the stars twinkled brightly in the sky. Nobody spoke as they sat and looked into the fire, thinking about what had just happened. What they failed to notice was that Dr Miles was also gone. He had disappeared during the gunfight with the fox. Jillian was the first to see he was gone and spoke up.

"Where's Peter?" she asked

They all looked around feverishly, trying to find some evidence of where he had gone. Tom got up from his seat and walked the perimeter of the camp, he noticed Peters hat on the floor and his jacket, there was also a small pool of blood towards the brush. Tom concluded that another fox had taken him. A noise caught his attention, he heard a rustle in the bushes behind him and turned to be confronted by a fox's snout, and it's dark eyes. He lifted his rifle under the fox's chin and fired off two rounds in quick succession, followed by David firing to the right at the fox's head. The fox jolted backwards, wobbling slightly before flopping to the floor by Tom's feet. Tom walked around the fox's snout and up to its eyes. He unloaded four rounds into the fox's head, ending its life once and for all. David walked up next to Tom and clasped him on the shoulder.

"Well done Tom," David said

"What about the other one" replied Tom

The other fox jumped the bushes right into the camp, clearing the campfire and scattering Rachel, Jillian, Julia, and Cameron. Tom and David opened fire with all they had, stunning the fox sending it retreating into the brush. Another gun opened fire, dropping the fox to the floor with a thud, it was Cameron. Both foxes now lay dead in the clearing. There was no way to move them, so they would have to move camp tomorrow.

"Anyone for fox steak?" said Cameron with a grin

"That was not appropriate, Cameron," said Rachel with her hands on her hips.

CHAPTER 9 – THE BIRTH

Saturday, November 16^{th,} 1991

Several years had now passed since getting lost in the wilds and losing General Hastings, Dr Strauss, Peter, and Doug. It was hard to keep motivated for a while, but survival was vital. They needed to get back to the Earth station, and every day meant one step closer, they hoped. Rachel was now pregnant with Cameron's child, and at least nine months along, she had quite the prominent belly, and Dr Peach had been preparing for this day for the two months. One of the tents was now a fully equipped maternity ward, makeshift from what they had but still pretty good. Jillian was looking forward to the birth. In all this madness, it was almost some normality.

Tom and David were out gathering supplies and searching the area for some clue to where they were in relation to the Earth station. The undergrowth and vegetation had changed considerably in the last few weeks, and Cameron was under the impression that this was a good thing. He believed with the brush thinning out. They could be nearing roads or maybe even a village. He was always optimistic even if the others weren't, much to their annoyance.

"Do you think we'll be out here forever?" asked David

"We, can't know at this point David, we have to keep trying" Tom replied

"I miss my car man," said David

"It's just a car!" said Tom sarcastically

"Shhh, you hear that," David said, holding his hand up.

In the distance was a low rumbling noise, two low rumbling noises, and they were getting closer to them. Tom rushed to the nearest tall bush he could find and began to climb it with David just behind. Using his hand to shield his eyes from the sun, he could make out a broad black line running through the trees and bushes. It wasn't too far away, only fifty or so meters, it was close. They would have passed right by it if they hadn't heard that rumbling thundering noise in the distance. Tom slipped down to the ground and made off towards what could only be a road. David was taken back but ran after him as best he could.

"What is it man" David shouted after Tom

"The road, it's the road," he replied.

Tom skidded to a halt at the edge of the tarmac. He could hardly believe his eyes. For eleven years, they had been searching, and they had finally found it, after all this time. He was in shock almost frozen to the spot until David came barrelling into the back of him at a full run. They both tumbled to the floor in a heap on the edge of the asphalt. Neither of them had heard that the rumbling in the distance was almost upon them. It was two chopper-style motorbikes. Both bikes were gleaming in the sunlight, the chrome on them glinting like polished mirrors. On top of the bikes were two men, tattoos up and down their arms, one had long hair and a beard the other short hair and piercings. They were cruising steadily along the road with their bikes chugging rhythmically and slight grins on their faces.

"Oliver, how much farther bud" shouted the smaller of the two

"About twenty miles Deano" replied the bearded one

Tom and David watched the two bikes go past throbbing and vibrating the ground under them. There was no way of getting their attention. Tom jumped up quickly and began waving his arms frantically and calling out. David didn't move; in awe of what he had just seen, he almost didn't believe what he was seeing. Dean looked in his left rear-view mirror and noticed what he thought was an action man dancing in the road behind him. Dean shook his head and carried on cruising. He was seeing things again. Dean knew he needed to lay off the cider for a while.

"Cameron, I think its time," said Rachel a little breathless

"It's only 3:30 hun, it's a bit early for tea," Replied Cameron looking at the map he had been making.

"My waters broke you prat," said Rachel

"Oh my," said Cameron

Tom and David arrived breathless coming through the perimeter, clumsily and loudly. They had been running for the best part of an hour and were so out of breath they could barely speak.

"Ruh, Ruh, Ruh, Road" Tom Managed

"Shut up, Tom. She's having the baby" said Julia

Inside the makeshift ward, they could hear the whimpers and cries of Rachel giving birth. All of them could overhear the sounds of Dr Peach bustling around in the tent. They all waited patiently for the delivery of the baby, it was a miracle in this awful situation, and it gave them all hope. Hope that was needed, desperately, hope that finding the road would lead them back to the earth station. Tom and David finding the tarmac road was now forgotten, the new-born was now the priority. A few moments passed, and all was quiet in the tent, Tom and David could hear talking and laboured breathing but not much else. A loud groan came from the shelter as Rachel began to push. It lasted a lifetime, and everyone was holding their breath for her.

A few hours passed, and now the contractions were getting closer together with every minute. They knew that the baby would be here at any moment; the anticipation was driving them all crazy. A loud groan and strain from Rachel came from the tent, followed by an infant crying that all too familiar cry of a new-born baby. Relief washed over everyone in the camp, to hear that little one cry out was a miracle in itself. Joy was spreading through the camp, which uplifted everyone's spirits; the baby was a little girl. When Dr Peach showed Rachel her baby, she began to cry tears of joy and happiness, Cameron too was weeping and so was the baby. One by one, they entered the tent to greet the little one and give gifts that they had made from wood and stones or from what they had salvaged along the way. Rachel and Cameron had named the baby Rosie due to the rosiness of her cheeks when she came into this world and a fitting name it was.

That evening they sat around the campfire in awe of little Rosie and the miracle of childbirth, especially being lost out on the wilderness. It was quiet, and all of them were gazing at the baby and thinking of the years to come. That's when Tom remembered the road and spoke up, breaking the silence like a well-timed drum solo.

"We've found the road," he said, louder than he expected.

Everyone turned their faces and looked directly at him.

"What do you mean?" asked Cameron

"We've found the road it's about half a day's walk towards the morning sun" he replied

"We've found it," he continued.

Everyone was elated by this news, and combined with the birth of Rosie. They couldn't be happier. They were finally on the right track or road.

CHAPTER 10 – CHILD NUMBER 2

Friday, August 23rd, 1992

Tracking the road was easy, staying safe and out of sight was the real problem. The group had to stay in the undergrowth as much as possible. They were staying hidden from potential dangers like traffic or animals. Not much traffic passed, the odd car but the road was mostly quiet. Tom realised that this was a private road and not a public highway. There were no markings on it, no drainage, and no road signs. They hoped that it led to a farm or even the earth station, but there was no way of knowing at this point. Travelling with a baby was slowing them down, but there was no way they were leaving anyone behind.

On top of that, Rachel was again pregnant, due sometime in December. Generally, the group thought Cameron should try and keep it in his trousers, but they were a couple, and they did those couple things together. There was no birth control here or contraceptives, it was the natural order of things. This time though Rachel was struggling with the pregnancy, it was unclear how this one would turn out. They were lucky with Rosie.

With the camp set up under an outcrop of rocks a few yards from the road, they intended to stay put now until the baby was born. Dr Peach didn't want to risk anything happening to Rachel and Rosie. It was the sensible option as winter was coming fast, and they needed somewhere warm and dry for when the baby came.

Rosie was as cute as a button and an extremely happy child,

so easily pleased, which made looking after her a doddle. They all took their turn in watching her, even David, who thought she was about the most fantastic thing he had ever seen. The camp was ready before nightfall with three tents, one for the family, one for medical and one for the others. Tom and Jillian had grown very close and pretty much were a couple, though they had not officially told anyone. They would sneak off for an hour here and there and do couples things in the bushes. Julia Hoffman had grown very distant, except when around Rosie, she would barely speak and would disappear for hours at a time. When confronted about it, she would say she was taking in the beautiful scenery. Everybody dealt with the isolation in their way. The group figured this was her way of doing it.

The baby came into the world on Christmas day 1992 at 11 am. It was a boy, healthy and strong with piercing blue eyes and a full head of hair. The labour was half the time that Rosie took to come into the world, and he was just as cute. Cameron and Rachel named him Benjamin after Cameron's father. Rachel did not fare so well this time and had to have help with the birth from Dr Peach. It meant that she would not be able to have any more children in the future. Dr Peach had to perform a hysterectomy after the birth due to the excessive bleeding. Cameron had thought he was going to lose his wife, but thanks to the efforts of Dr Peach, she pulled through. The field medic training and the supplies saved from the carrier had made all the difference to a situation that could have gone very bad.

January 1st, 1993

Tom and David were still doing their rounds in the day looking for the earth station and some sign that they were heading in the right direction. The hope was dwindling in their minds, and it got harder and harder to press on. Thirteen years was a long time to be isolated with only five other people around. The two children helped, but that only went so far. After finding the road, everyone's spirit had perked up. They were motivated to move on, but now that spirit had dwindled to dim candlelight in a pitch-black room.

David was absent-mindedly kicking small pebbles along the side of the road. Cars would flit past at what looked like two hundred miles an hour, and they couldn't even see the people inside due to being so small. The cars only came on the odd occasion. Otherwise, it was just an empty stretch of road. One way was foliage, trees, and a tarmac strip, and the other way was foliage trees and a tarmac strip. The tarmac looked like a huge leather belt around the world they currently knew, and David couldn't decide whether they were on the top half of the body or the bottom. At least it was clearer today, it was almost always damp, foggy or raining, so visibility was minimal at best. Today though, you could see for miles and miles, though there was nothing to see. David stood up straight like a meerkat on a hill. He could see something in the distance, something big, a building he thought. If only David had some binoculars or a telescope, but no such luck out here. He could hear Tom rustling around behind him, so he called him over.

"Tom look at this," he said pointing at the object in the distance

"What is it?" Tom asked

"I think it's a building."

"I think your right man."

"We need to tell the others; how far do you think it is?"

"It's miles away, but it's a heading."

They made their way back to the camp with the news, hopeful it would lift everyone's spirits. This good news was what the group needed. This time they didn't run back to the camp. The years had made them realise they needed to conserve their energy for anything that may lie ahead. It was a two-hour walk back to camp, and they needed to be back before dark, so had to pick up the pace. The trail was relatively treacherous and would be hard going with the children coming along. Arriving back at the camp, they organised a group meeting to discuss their findings.

> After discussions that evening on how to progress towards the building in the distance, it was decided that they would stay put for a couple of weeks while they formulated a plan. They had been out here for Thirteen years so far and didn't think a couple of extra weeks would hurt. They did, however, discuss the idea that David and Tom would scout on ahead and see how far away the building was. They would do this in a week's time, be back within a week, and report back their findings. One troubling issue to the group was the ever-lengthening disappearances of Julia and the fact that it was becoming more frequent. She was distancing herself from the group and becoming more and more distant in herself. It was a bit of an elephant in the room, but Jillian was becoming concerned for her wellbeing and believed it was time to discuss it. Julia wasn't even there for this meeting, so she wouldn't even know the plans for the coming weeks. If they left, they might lose her. Cameron decided it was time to confront her and see what was going on, no one wanted to interfere, but something had to change.

> Julia arrived back at the camp late and disappeared straight to bed before Cameron could confront her. She was unaware of everyone staring at her as she re-entered the campsite. She was almost in a trance being controlled and directed to the sleeping tent. Cameron decided to let it be for now until the morning came, and everyone had gotten some sleep.

CHAPTER 11 - JULIA HOFFMAN

Friday, August 23rd, 1993

Julia was lying in bed, her mind unravelling from the day and exhaustion setting in. She didn't even know how long she had been away. Julia hadn't known she was descending into a pit of madness. First, she was just scared to be out there all alone with people she barely knew, but once the madness had taken hold of her, she had stopped caring. Julia believed that they were all going to die out here and never return to the Earth station. It started as fear and made her very nervous. The slightest noise and she would jump out of her skin, an animal nearby, and she would freak out. For the first few years, she lived in fear of everything out here but couldn't show it being the second in command. She barely slept, she barely ate, and she rarely spoke to any of the group. As the years went on, Julia started to feel separated from the group. At one point, she believed that they were going to do something to her. It made her crazier, and Julia wouldn't turn her back on anyone. By the late 80's she had decided to break away from the group fearing they would doing something to her. She was leaving for longer and longer periods, returning only due to hunger or fear of an animal attack.

Soon the fear developed so much it no longer felt real, and she started to dismiss it as her imagination. The dream state made it very dangerous for her and meant she took multiple risks every day. Julia believed that it was all a dream, and she could not get hurt. She would climb plants and bushes and then jump down without a care in the world. Julia would walk straight up to insects and touch them, eat berries and flowers without knowing what they were. She started to look at the world differently, almost as if she was in a dream. Julia was talking to the insects and the birds, and they were answering back in her mind. Deep down, she knew she was losing the plot, but it was better than being afraid all the time.

Julia was all alone in the wilderness. She had wandered off this morning with no particular direction in mind. The sun was shining, and the wilderness looked beautiful in the sun's rays. The flowers were all manner of colours brightly shining in the daylight; they were the size of umbrellas to her. She danced her way through the wildflowers, dancing like no one was watching. She wandered up to the roadway and looked at the dark black tarmac in front of her. Julia walked out slowly onto the tarmac to see what was there, the other side looking far away but inviting. She decided to cross and see what was on the other side. Halfway across the road, Julia felt a rumbling noise to her right. Two large motorcycles came thundering towards her, the two men on them talking to each other, not noticing she was there.

"Been a few years since we've been down here?" said Dean

"Yeah mate, way too long" replied Oliver

Julia crouched down and put her hands over here head and brought her knees to her chest like a fetal position and closed her eyes. The Fear was burning up inside her again. It seemed so real compared to the rest of the dream; she had a momentary lapse in her madness and found her sanity. The two motorbikes spilt around her as they carried on along the road, she jumped up and ran to the other side of the road diving into a nearby bush. One of the bikers looked over his shoulder back the way they had come. He frowned, not that you could tell through his large sunglasses, and turned back to the way he was going. He shook his head and said nothing to the other biker; they just carried on.

Julia was now on the other side of the road. The foliage was different here, almost kept and trimmed. Squeezing through the tall grass and down the bank, she came out into a grassy field with hedged borders and cows grazing in it. For a moment she was stunned, astonished to see cattle, and then she fell to her bum on the ground and put her head in her hands.

"This can't be real we haven't seen cows since we've been here," she thought

The dream-like feeling started to come back to her. She was dreaming again; it couldn't be real. Julia looked up to see one of the cows coming over. It was quite interested in Julia getting closer every second. They were all talking in groups in the field, it reminded her of a school playground, with different groups of friends talking together. One cow had now meandered up near to her; the sheer size of the cow was enough to petrify Julia. They were big enough when you were five foot ten but being less than six inches tall, they were monstrous. Julia's sanity came flooding back, this was very real right now, and she backed away through the long grass and up the bank to the road. She could feel the weight of the cow thudding through the floor under her feet. She paused and looked at the road, looked both ways, and ran across the road without hesitation, hoping to make it across. Julia crashed through the bushes and ran into the undergrowth, making her way back to the camp. It was late, and the night was coming in, she needed to head for shelter quick.

Julia made it to the outskirts of the camp, she needed to tell them about the cattle and the motorbikes, tell them what had happened to her. Tell them she was ok now and was sorry for being crazy and disappearing. Julia wanted to see the children, she wished to hold the baby, and most of all, Julia wanted to be part of the group. Julia knew she was the reason for her exile. It was all in her head, but now she felt normal again. She made her way up to the camp and could hear the group talking. They were talking about something important, and they were talking about her.

"We need to confront Julia," Cameron was saying, "This has gong on long enough now."

Julia froze, they were out to get her, they were going to kill her. She needed to get back to her bed and hideaway. Julia would leave again in the morning and not come back. She waited until the group had dispersed and made her way to the sleeping tent, not looking at anyone and keeping a straight line to her bed. Julia entered the tent, which was empty, and removed her jacket and trousers. She was stick thin, as she barely ate anything you could see all her muscles, her washboard abs, and her breasts stuck out like grapefruits on her chest. Her underwear was hanging off her around her waist and the tops of her legs, the only thing fitting tight was her bra due to her ample chest. Her underwear was worn beige and mismatched with multiple repairs to them. She got into bed and pulled the blankets up over her head to hide. The lack of nutrition and the amount of running she and done today had made her extremely tired, so she was fighting herself to stay awake. Her eyes were heavy, and her body felt like lead in the bed. She would be asleep soon, no doubt about it.

A few minutes passed, and she was drifting away into sleep when she heard footsteps coming into the tent, followed by the feeling of a person standing over her. Was this it, they were going to end her in her sleep, her eyes burst open with adrenaline, and her breath quickened. She threw off the blankets and jumped out of bed. Standing in front of her was Rachel holding a small bundle in her arms, which was making cute gurgling noises. Julia stopped, and confusion washed over her, what was going on, she expected to see Cameron or David with a gun or at least a knife or something. Rachel smiled at her. She pulled the blankets on the bundle down and showed Julia the face of a handsome baby boy.

"He likes you know," Rachel said softly "He cries at most of the others, put some clothes on, we need to talk Julia."

Julia pulled on here dirty cargo trousers and slipped her jumper over her head. She sat on her bed, looking at Rachel and the baby in silence for a while as Rachel sat down and settled Benjamin. Julia couldn't help but smile at the boy. He was gorgeous. She had always wanted kids of her own but never found the right partner, and out here, she probably never would. The only free man she could be with would be David, and she could barely stand him as a work colleague, a lover would be a definite no. Rachel was looking at Julia solemnly, and she broke a smile before she spoke to her.

"We're all anxious about you, Julia, we hadn't said anything before as we thought you'd come around in time. It's been years now, and it wasn't too bad at first, but lately, you disappear for hours, even days. Where do you go?" Rachel said quietly.

Julia sat silently on the bed, not taking her eyes off Benjamin. She smiled and loosened up a little and then looked up to Rachel tears in her eyes. She reached out towards Benjamin, looking into Rachel's eyes.

"Please may I hold him" Julia Asked

Rachel was taken back a bit and was hesitant at first but then conceded and passed little Benjamin across to Julia. Julia held him carefully and close to her chest. She held him gently, and it brought a big smile to her face. She relaxed into herself and glanced up at Rachel.

"He's beautiful. He's so little and sweet. It amazes me how children come into this world. You must be so proud." Julia said smiling

"He's wonderful isn't he, you could have held him sooner you know, and you could have held Rosie too, you were just so distant from us all" Rachel replied

"I know, I got so scared and couldn't deal with all this, it drove me insane. I thought this was all a dream. The scare I had today woke me from that, and I think I'm in a better place now."

"There's no rush, Julia, just know we are here for you, we are all here for you."

"I'm sorry for any trouble I've caused Rachel."

"It's fine, Julia, now let's go and see the others."

Rachel stood and headed for the entrance of the tent. Julia did the same but paused and looked at Rachel. She held out Benjamin for her to take, but Rachel shook her head.

"You can bring him with you."

They both walked out of the tent, Julia holding Benjamin and Rachel walking alongside. They headed for the campfire. The others were waiting sat around the fire, chatting amongst themselves. They saw Julia and Rachel coming, and all stood to greet them. Each of them hugged Julia and welcomed her back to the group. They were all so pleased to see her. Julia felt a tremendous weight lifted off her; she felt set free. She then remembered the field of cattle and the events of the day and explained what she had found on the other side of the road.

CHAPTER 12 – THE BARN

Sunday, May 28^{th,} 2000

Seven years had passed, and the road hadn't produced anything yet. They did stay put for a while due to the children and Rachel's health, but now Rachel was fit and fully recovered; her mum's duties keeping her active. They had been a handful, but both children were healthy and bright and eager to learn all about the world. Cameron and Dr Peach had been giving them lessons four times a day, like a school. Keeping them near the camp was the hardest part; they were so curious about the world around them. Being the start of the new millennium, they decide at a group meeting that it was time to press on toward the Earth station. They had now been lost for twenty years, and it was getting harder and harder to stay hopeful. The two children helped take their minds off things, but that only went so far. The group had checked out the field and the cow's, but it was no help to them. For all they knew, the farm was twenty miles away or more. The cows seemed huge and would be of no use to them. They had no way to milk them or kill them for beef.

The building that David had seen was now only yards away, and they were all excited to find it and see what it was. They could see it was built from concrete blocks and corrugated roofing sheets. Tom believed it was a hay barn or maybe a cowshed. They would find out tomorrow.

Monday, May 29^{th,} 2000

They were all up early, and today was the day they would reach the building. Cameron, Tom, and David started to pack up the tents, and by midday, they were off into the wilderness. They reached the building at five pm, it loomed over them like a sky-scraper, blotting out the sun. Tom and David made their way around the other side of the building to find the entrance, telling the others to wait and stay out of sight. When they reached the other side, they found it was an empty hay barn, and it looked as though it hadn't been used for years. David returned to the rest of the group and got them to follow him around to the front.

"It's just a barn then," said Rachel

"It's evidence of civilisation is what it is" replied Cameron

"We should camp here for a few days and see if we can get our bearings," said Tom "If we can get up on the roof, we might be able to see the Earth station."

They set up camp in one corner of the inside of the Barn. It was the first time they have had proper shelter in twenty years. The tents were erected, and a campfire lit in the middle, ready for supper. Both children were playing amongst some left-over hay, trying to build a fort out of it. Tom and David were now looking for a way to climb up the building so they could get a view of their surroundings. They decided to use the old drainpipe at the rear and would give it a go in the morning.

Night came quickly, and they all settled for the night, both kids were asleep, and the others were in their beds waiting for sleep to take them. Noises were coming from the other side of the barn, squeaking, getting louder by the minute. Tom sat up in bed. He knew what it was; they should have checked for rats but were too busy deciding how to climb the building. Tom grabbed his rifle and ran out of the tent, bumping into David on the way. He was also holding his gun. They nodded to each other and went outside. They couldn't see anything, but there was a definite rustling coming their way. Tom grabbed a stick from the fire and held it out towards the noise, illuminating two large front teeth and a set of twitching whiskers. In front of them was a giant rat, the size of a horse to them, with dark grey fur and black eyes. It didn't like the fire and drew back, the flames flickered in its eyes like yellow suns. It was making a low squeaking sound and twitching ever so slightly. It was almost mesmerised by the fire. Tom and David stood their ground and attempted to push the rat backwards away from camp with torches from the campfire. It was working so far; the fire was scaring it off and forcing it to retreat. A small gust of wind blew through the barn and blew out Tom and David's torches. The rat shrieked and began to run at them, they both threw the torches to the floor and bolted for the campfire. The rat had now cornered them in their camp, still wary of the campfire but aggressive enough to keep pushing forward. As they moved with the rat trying to keep it at bay, Rachel emerged from one of the tents to see what was happening. She was holding Benjamin in her arms, and Rosie was next to her holding her trouser leg. The Rat lunged for the three of them, jumping the campfire and landing in front of Rachel.

"No" shouted Cameron dashing toward the rat

From their left came a mighty roar, and a figure jumped from the side of the barn, landing on the rat's neck and holding a makeshift spear. It was Julia, she was enraged. She stabbed the rat in the back of the neck. The rat thrashed around, throwing Julia like a rag doll, but she held fast. It tried to jump the campfire and head for the grass, but Julia was already thrusting the spear into it, penetrating it before the rat could escape. It slid into its eyeball with Julia putting all her weight on it pushing it deep into the rat's head. The rat dropped to the floor, lifeless and limp with a spear sticking out of its head, and Julia Hoffman stood on top.

"We are so glad you are back Julia," said Rachel with a proud smile

"Remind me not piss you off," said David

Julia shot David a glare but softened and smiled at him. She felt good, she felt semi-normal, and she felt like a real part of the group for the first time.

Tuesday, May 30^{th,} 2000

Morning came quickly, but they were up and anxious to see what was in view from atop the hay barn. David had run the last night shift, so he was asleep in one of the tents snoring loudly.

Tom was gathering the rope and climbing axes from the supplies they had salvaged from the carrier years before. The group had elected Tom to be the one to climb the barn and see what he could see. He was the most qualified for the job, and with his upper body strength, it should be a cinch. Tom made his way around to the cast iron drainpipe at the rear of the building, followed by Julia. They stopped at the drainpipe. Tom put the rope down and climbing axe down. Tom turned to Julia and put a hand on her shoulder.

"Your, in charge of security while I'm gone," Tom said handing her his rifle

"You might need that" she replied

"It'll only slow me down," he replied

He put the coil of rope over his head and one shoulder and picked up the climbing axes, gave Julia a short salute and began climbing the downpipe.

It took Tom four hours to reach the top of the barn. He stopped every hour to regain some strength, drink, and eat something. It was a clear day, and he could still see Julia at the bottom of the drainpipe, he gave her a wave, and she waved back. Tom then disappeared from view and walked along to the middle of the roof. He put down his gear and took a look around, it was extra bright and sunny today, and he could see for miles. Looking to the rear of the barn, he could make out the sea. To the left were trees, grass fields, and brush. To his right was the road and the cattle fields. He looked to the front of the barn, and in the distance, he could see Arthur the massive twenty-six-meter satellite dish at Goonhilly Earth station. It took his breath away; he fell to his knees and began to cry tears of joy. For twenty years, they have been looking for Goonhilly Earth station, and today they had finally found it. It was several miles away, and it would take a few years to get there, but they saw it, they finally found it. Tom was ecstatic and couldn't wait to get back down and tell the great news. A rumbling noise in the distance caught his attention, to his right. He looked out and, in the distance, he saw two motorcycles gleaming in the sun, it was like a premonition or a sign, they were cruising along the tarmac road toward the Earth station. They were going to get home, for the first time in years he finally believed that.

After an hour of taking in the views and staring at Arthur, Tom started to make his descent using the rope to get as far down as he could and the axes to steady his progress. It only took two hours until he was on the ground again, there was no one there to greet him, but he didn't care. He ran around to the campfire and shouted aloud the great news; everybody came to greet him. They cried, they laughed, they hugged, and they knew that they were on their way back. That evening they sat around the campfire telling stories, laughing and joking, eating, and drinking. It was the happiest they had been in a long time, but they all knew the journey ahead would start tomorrow and who knew what it would bring them.

PART 4

CHAPTER 13 – THE WAY HOME

Thursday, August 12^{th,} 2010

"I do love it when you tell that story, darling," said Rachel, handing out cups of tea.

"It changes every time," said Benjamin.

They were all sat around the campfire listening to Cameron tell their life story, they all knew it, of course, but they loved the way he spun it. There was excitement in the group. They had made their way along the side of the road and could see Arthur in the distance on a clear day getting closer with every step. They had a heading and were making a good pace; it wouldn't be long now. Tom believed they would reach the earth station by the end of the month, as the progress was so good. The journey had been hard and dangerous as expected, but with Julia on board, nothing could stop them. They were a close-knit team, and the children being in their late teens now were as big a part of the group as anyone. Each of them had their role to play, and they all played their roles perfectly.

Tom and Jillian were now closer than ever, although still hiding their relationship, they were getting pretty open about it. They were also in charge of security now, and that gave them a lot of alone time. Rachel and Cameron were given the task of food and supplies, along with help from David. Ben and Rosie were in charge of water supply and keeping it clean and fresh, and they also collected up firewood for the campfire.

The squirrel had been following them for a while now. Although it didn't come close, Ben knew it was there. Every so often, Ben would coax the squirrel close and feed him. He was getting pretty tame. Rosie knew all of this but kept it a secret like Ben as she thought the squirrel was cute, and it was fun to be around. Ben was still planning to ride it like a horse, but after the last time, he was slightly apprehensive. This particular night though, they hadn't seen the squirrel, which they had aptly names Nutz, which was unusual. It was a wild animal, though, and not a pet Labrador. Ben was sure Nutz would turn up at some point, he was probably off seeing his girlfriends or something.

Wednesday, August 25^{th,} 2010

A week had passed by, and they could now read the signs on the fences and could make out the other satellite dishes. They were so close now; the satellite dishes would block out the sun, and they could see the barbed wire on the fences. They decided to camp one more night out in the wild before they entered the Earth station. They were excited but were all exhausted from the constant travelling. They set up camp below one of the walls on the perimeter of the Earth station. There was a hollow in the wall that worked perfectly as shelter. They decided only to set up one tent and all sleep together tonight. They had no idea what was out there or in the Earth Station.

"In the morning, we will climb up the wall and through the chain-link fence. The links should be big enough to climb through" said Tom

"What if the fence is electrified?" asked Cameron

"We will tackle that in the morning, at this point it's an unknown" replied Tom

"We stick together and stay low," said David

"Everybody knows that we were chased off from the Station, so we don't know what welcome we would get," added Tom.

"We should get some sleep," said Rachel. "It's a big day tomorrow."

They were all tucked up in their blankets in a row inside the tent. Rachel, Cameron, Ben, and Rosie together one side of the tent and the others on the other side. Tom and Jillian slept together, they still denied their relationship, but it was so obvious now. Julia and David were already asleep with their backs to each other; no love lost there,

"What do you think is in their Ben" whispered Rosie

"I don't know Rosie, but tomorrow we should find out," replied Ben.

That night Ben was woken up by a sniffing noise and a rustling, he climbed out of his bed and pulled the tent doors slightly apart, peaking out. In front of him was Nutz, the Squirrel, sat very much like a dog and nearly panting like one. Ben was a bit surprised but also pleased to see him. He was wondering where he had gone. Ben felt someone behind him and then saw a black gun barrel slide over his shoulder.

"Don't move Ben" said Tom quietly but loud enough to sound serious

"No don't, it's not going to hurt us," said Ben in a panic

He jumped out of the tent and stood in front of the squirrel blocking Tom's shot, Nutz was tilting his head and looking at Tom.

"Move Boy" growled Tom

"No this is Nutz, and he's my friend or umm pet" shouted, Ben

"Is this the squirrel you tried to ride?" asked Cameron emerging from the tent "Fascinating, it's not even scared. It's like a pet dog or something."

Ben moved back towards the squirrel and bumped into it, the squirrel didn't move and just looked at him with black eyes. The squirrel then nuzzled Ben's neck, making a kind of cooing noise. Tom and Cameron looked at each other and burst out laughing. They had never seen anything so hilarious in their lives.

"What's going on," asked Rachel poking her head out of the tent. "Oh my".

"Looks like you got a friend for life their pal," said David

"Can we keep him?" Rosie asked trying to be cute

"Well if it wants to stay, it can I suppose, the first sign of trouble though and I'll have to shoot it," said Tom

"He'll be fine, his names Nutz" replied Ben

They all started laughing again and went back into the tent. Ben remained outside and petted the squirrel for a bit before returning to the tent. Nutz tried to follow, but Ben stopped him and told him to lie by the tent, which the squirrel duly did, to Ben's amazement. Ben slipped back into the tent, and under his blankets, he couldn't help but wonder if the squirrel would be there in the morning or not.

CHAPTER 14 – IN ARTHURS SHADOW

Thursday, August 26ᵗʰ, 2010

The group awoke to birds singing in the distance and bright sunlight coming through the gap in the tent entrance. Tom was already pulling his boots on ready to go outside, but Ben barged past and out the flaps. He looked around frantically, but the squirrel was gone, he wasn't surprised just sad that Nutz didn't hang around.

"I have a feeling he will be back," said Tom clasping a hand on Ben's shoulder.

They decided to leave the camp set up and return for it later if they needed to, this would lighten their load for the journey ahead. In the daylight, they could make out the sheer height of the fence and the wall. They weren't going to be able to climb it. Scanning along the wall, Tom noticed several round openings for drainage. He climbed up to one of them and peered inside, it was dead straight and only as long as the wall was thick. It was perfect for them to walk through at about six inches in diameter. He sent down a climbing rope, and they all made their way up into the drainpipe or to them a tunnel. Carefully they made their way up the tunnel and came out on a tarmacked car park, semi overgrown with weeds, but they recognised it straight away. They were not far from the hanger where the ship was. It was open terrain, so they would have to be quick to cross it with the birds that were circling overhead. The place looked almost abandoned like no one had been here for many years; the doors to the hanger were chained up. They decided they would cross in groups of two and meet at the hanger doors. It took about half an hour to accomplish, but luckily there were no incidents from the bird's overhead.

At the entrance to the hanger, the doors were locked up with a heavy chain and a substantial armoured padlock. They hadn't opened in years, but there was enough space between the doors to squeeze through. What they failed to notice was the CCTV cameras above them pointing right at them. They squeezed through one by one into the darkness on the other side of the doors. They were back in the grey hallway. It was surreal to be back in this hallway where they had been thirty years ago. The bank vault style door was wide open and looked to have not shut since they left. They hugged the wall as they made their way to the entrance to the main hanger, these doors were wide open, and there was a slight glow of light coming through them. Tom reached the door jamb first and looked around into the hanger and, to his surprise, saw the Goon sat on the supports where they left it all those years ago. There was even light emitting from the windows and the open cargo door on the ship. Tom waved at them, gesturing for them to follow him. They made their way across to the ship and met at the base. The ladder on the side of the frame was their scale and built for them to use. One by one, they made their way up the ladder and on to the platform meeting at the open cargo doors.

"It's still here. I can't believe it" said, Cameron

"Yeah, and it's still powered up," said David "That's weird."

A familiar voice with a German accent greeted them at the top of the loading ramp.

"Weird, you say, what's weird is you are all alive," said Dr Strauss

"Oh my god," said Jillian, "Dr Strauss, you're alive."

"Older but very much alive my dear" he replied

Jillian ran up the ramp and hugged him before breaking it off abruptly and apologising.

"You must come on board quickly," Dr Strauss ushered

them inside. "Please follow me up to the bridge."

They all followed Dr Strauss up to the lift and boarded together, Dr Strauss pressing the button for the bridge and the doors sliding shut. Tom looked at Cameron and sniggered.

"You still not keen on lifts Dr Strauss?" asked Cameron

"I am quite fine thank you" he replied

They all burst out laughing at once, even Dr Strauss, Rosie and Ben were very confused, what was so funny. The elevator dinged and the doors opened to the bridge, one by one they exited the elevator and gathered around the captain's chair. There were two other people on board in white lab coats, one male, one female.

"Allow me to introduce Dr Franks and Dr Heals. They were working with me on the construction of the ship. And I see you have two new comrades as well" said, Dr Strauss

"These are our children, Rosie and Ben," said Rachel holding Cameron's arm

"Well, Well, you have been busy, pleased to meet you," replied Dr Strauss.

"We thought you were dead," said Julia

"I thought the same of all of you, though I don't see Mr Bolaski or Dr Miles?" Dr Strauss asked

"They didn't make it, and neither did General Hastings" answered Tom

"let me explain what happened here, and then you can tell us your story," said Dr Strauss

They all took a seat, and Dr Strauss began to explain what happened.

"When I last saw you all you were being carried away by General Hastings, I fell out of the carrier and hit the ground quite hard, so hard I broke my leg. In the panic, I slowly made my way back into the hanger and back onto the ship. I closed the cargo door and locked it shut, locking myself and my two colleagues here inside. We assumed a low profile and rigged the ship to run silently while we hid away inside. The government searched this place high and low for five years before eventually giving up. Because we had all these supplies onboard, it was relatively easy to wait them out. The agents decided this was a scale model of what we were building and didn't pay us much attention. Finally, after five years, they locked the doors and put a small security detail on this place, and its been like it ever since. We do venture out occasionally, but we found all we need here, so why risk it. We have been prepping for launch, but the three of us couldn't hope to pilot the Goon successfully. Now you're here though we can make this happen and escape this awful place. We saw you coming on the CCTV cameras, and that's when we knew we were going to be OK."

Dr Strauss sat back, noticeably satisfied with his story.

"You see, the whole point of the mission was to get into space quicker, traditional space travel is too slow. The main driver for this program was too colonize a new planet, and eventually, if this mission succeeded, we would shrink people and transport them to the new planet. Globally we know that the earth is dying, pollution is killing the planet, and fossil fuels are running out. It is estimated that the earth will be uninhabitable by the year 3000. When the army heard of my reduction machine, we collaborated on this project, and here we are today. Unfortunately, changes in Government staff didn't agree with our methods and were against using the reduction machine, calling it inhumane, and they would not support it. They believed that we could save the earth with changes to our way of life, but I'm afraid the earth is too far gone, and it would be impossible to undo what we have done to it."

"So, this was a one-way trip?" asked Cameron

"And we can't be un-shrunk then?" asked Julia

"No, no, it was a one-way trip. I'm afraid," replied Dr Strauss, "But you already knew that didn't you."

They all nodded in agreement, knowing this was the case but didn't want to believe it. It wouldn't matter if the team were normal-sized again anyway, the team would probably be declared legally dead by now. Cameron stood up suddenly, tripping over his own feet.

"Hang on, CCTV cameras?" asked Cameron

"Yes, we tapped into them when the agents put them up. Unfortunately, that does mean they saw you enter as well so are probably mobilizing to come here ASAP" replied Dr Strauss

"What's the plan, then doctor."

"We launch."

CHAPTER 15 – TIME TO FLY

Thursday, August 26^{th,} 2010

Dr Strauss and his team were prepared for the launch. They had prepped the ship and restocked from the supplies in the hanger. Dr Franks was now showing David the bridge and re-familiarizing him with the flight controls. Abigail Franks was a slight woman with long red hair and a freckled face. She and David had already exchanged several lustful glances. David found her very attractive, though being alone all this time who could blame him other than Jillian, there were no other women available. They carried on with the training, learning about the navigation system, the engines, and life support.

Dr Steven Heals was in the medical suite showing Dr Peach how the system works and state of the art (for 1980) machines. There was everything at her disposal from resuscitation machines to MRI scanners, fully stocked medicine cabinets, and several hospital beds. It had everything a hospital had and more, some of the equipment Julia had never seen in her life. Dr Heals was an older man in his sixties and balding on top. He was slightly camp in his speech and mannerisms and didn't hide the fact that he was gay. He was very open about it and did everything he could to remind people that he was. It got quite annoying, really, and Tom was getting very fed up with it. He had had enough and decided to head down to the armoury to see what he could find.

Ben and Rosie were still exploring the ship; they had been through the sleeping quarters and living areas and were now in the lift heading for the stores and biosphere. They didn't know what a biosphere was, and Rosie was extremely keen to find out. The elevator dinged on the fourth floor, and the doors opened with a swoosh to a wide-open space with crates and boxes stacked on all sides. Directly in front of them, about twenty meters away were a pair of glass doors to an airlock. To the right of these doors was a sign reading 'Biosphere', they had found it, and Rosie was ecstatic. Ben walked up to the doors and peered through them. He could see green vegetation and a light mist in the air. He went to try the doors but could find no handle or key-pad. There was only a blank, black glass panel. Rosie placed her hand on it, making it glow red and bleep displaying unauthorised. A voice with a distinct German accent came from behind them.

"I'm afraid your biometrics are not in the system young lady," said Dr Strauss

He walked forward and put a code into the panel, making a red handprint appear on the screen, the words calibrating was at the top of the screen.

"Place your fair hand on the scanner my dear" gestured Dr Strauss

Rosie placed her hand flat on the scanner, it bleeped, and the door opened with a swoosh. She removed her hand, and after a short period, the doors slid closed.

"Your turn Benjamin, can't leave you out," said Dr Strauss with a smile

Dr Strauss repeated the procedure, and Ben put his palm on the scanner. Once again, it bleeped, and the doors opened with a swoosh. Again, after a short while, the doors slid shut.

"There we go, that will give you access to all parts of the ship now, anywhere you find a scanner," said the doctor. "Now carry on and explore the biosphere. It's quite breathtaking".

"Thank you, Dr Strauss," said Ben, Rosie just remained quiet.

Rosie was a little wary of Dr Strauss. He seemed ok, but more than a little creepy. She was glad that Ben was with her and she wasn't alone with him. Dr Strauss left them at the entrance to the Biosphere and headed for the elevator. He entered and turned to face them and pushed the button inside, all the while staring at Rosie until the doors slid shut. Rosie shuddered and turned to

Ben. Ben was looking inside the Biosphere and about to put his hand on the scanner. When he did so, the doors opened, and they both stepped inside the airlock, the doors then sliding shut behind them. Two jets of what looked like steam sprayed them from the ceiling continued by a robotic voice saying:

"Decontamination complete."

The exit door of the airlock then slid open, slowly allowing them into what looked to be a rain forest with trees and plants they had never seen before. They walked through the vegetation in the Biosphere, and it was like being on another world. The moisture and heat in the air making beads of sweat run down their faces. From the trees hung different types of fruits that Ben and Rosie didn't recognise, long yellow fruits, orange fruits, and all manner of different kinds of nuts. Ben picked one of the yellow fruits and looked at it curiously. It was soft to the touch and squashy in his hands.

"That, son is a banana, you peel it and eat the inside," said Cameron from the entrance.

Ben did as his father said and shared the inside with Rosie, the taste explosion in their mouths was terrific; they had never eaten something so good. They were smiling ear to ear and eating the banana like it was going out of fashion.

"Come on, you two, we are getting ready to launch; you need to be on the bridge for this. We can come back here later," said Cameron, "take another each and let's go."

They both picked another banana and followed their father into the elevator, Cameron pushed the button for the bridge, and up they went.

Everyone had assembled on the bridge and were taking seats ready for the launch. Dr Strauss was doing the pre-flight checks at the command console and prepping the engines while Dr Heals was watching the CCTV at the security console. Keeping an eye for any agents that may be coming, so far, they hadn't seen anyone. Dr Strauss was sure they would arrive any minute, but in the last eight hours, they had not seen anyone. Rachel was securing her children in some flight chairs at the rear of the bridge. The others were securing themselves as well.

"Dr Strauss, the government, has arrived in several black trucks, they have rammed the gate and are heading our way," Dr Heals called out across the bridge.

"That's it then, open the roof and start the nuclear engines," said Dr Strauss. "Its time to light this candle."

Dr Franks pressed a button on her console, and outside the ship, they could hear mechanisms working above the ship, she pressed another button, and the ship viewport flickered into a view of the roof of the hanger. The roof was separating above them, dust and rubbish were floating down on the ship from above. They could see the night sky above them appear through the gap. It was drizzling down on the ship, and droplets were running down the camera feeding the screen. Dr Strauss sat into a captain's chair and strapped in. They were all now strapped into chairs as the ship began to rise upward, pointing vertically to the roof and pushing them all back into their chairs. They could hear things creaking and moving inside the ship as it continued to rise and finally resting in a vertical position. There was a hum from the base of the ship getting louder every second and making the ship vibrate. The screen now flicked to the CCTV footage, and they could see the agents cutting of the heavy chains and padlock on the entrance door, frantically trying to get in.

"Changing that lock was a brilliant idea Dr Franks" shouted Dr Strauss. "Over to you, Captain Beckett."

"Countdown to ignition on screen please," said David

The screen flicked back to the view of the night sky with a countdown timer in the bottom right corner.

"Five, Four, Three, Two, One, punch it Julia" commanded David

Agents were now entering the hanger when suddenly a burst of energy from the ship's engines blasted them backwards. It sent them out of the doors and back into the hallway. The ship lurched forward and began to rise, getting quicker and quicker, appearing through the roof within a couple of seconds and blasting upwards at a surprising speed disappearing into the night sky in a blur. Everyone was hanging on to their chairs on the bridge, grimacing at the sheer velocity they were travelling. Within minutes they had burst through the atmosphere, and the speed they were travelling did not appear so fast. The ship began to settle out and cruise through the blackness, the screen showing the vastness of space in front of them. They were all amazed into silence, speechless, and in awe of where they had found themselves.

Dr Franks turned the screen to the rear camera, and they could all see the earth shrinking behind them as they travelled deeper into space. Their home planet looked so different, so blue so strange from this vantage point. As they drew farther away, it was nothing spectacular in the view screen, just a small planet.

PART 5

CHAPTER 16 – GOON MK1

Monday, August 22^{nd,} 2011 (Mission Date 361)

Nearly a year has passed since leaving the earth, they had travelled into outer space passing Voyager 1 just yesterday and now into unexplored territory. They all now have their roles on the ship, Rosie and Ben included, Rosie was working with Dr Peach and Ben training with Tom.

In the armoury, Tom was showing Ben the weapons available, machine guns, rifles, and handguns. Ben had become quite the shot, dead centre of all targets in the shooting range and was giving Tom a real run for his money. Rachel was not too keen on the fact that he had been learning how to use weapons and learning how to fight, Cameron, on the other hand, couldn't be prouder. Rosie was learning everything she could from Jillian. She was quite the hands-on nurse now, Rachel was incredibly proud of her.

"Do you think we will find any inhabitable planets out there, doctor?" Julia asked Dr Strauss

"We can only hope, but you'd be a fool to think that we had the only planet like ours," he replied.

"We will find something, I'm sure," said David.

Rosie was in the Biosphere admiring the plants and trees as she did most days, if you couldn't find her on the ship, that's where she would be. She was still very fond of bananas and would eat at least one every day. She was sat under a banana tree right now eating one. She had become a gorgeous young woman, with the fresh clothing and doctor's lab coat she was so striking to look at. Any young man would be proud to be her partner and would be hard-pressed to find any better.

The doors to the biodome slid open, and Dr Strauss walked in, he still made Rosie very nervous, especially when on her own, so she decided to hide behind the trees rather than have to talk to him. He was carrying what looked like an electronic clipboard and ticking off inventory. She stayed very still as he walked past her and put her hand over her mouth so he couldn't hear her breathe. Dr Strauss paused by the tree she was hiding behind and then walked off in the direction of the entrance. She breathed a sigh of relief and relaxed, although he was an older man in his late sixties, he still scared her.

"Hello Rosie," said Dr Strauss, clasping a hand on her shoulder. "Are you hiding from me."

Rosie squirmed as he pulled her up off the floor and continued to hold her by the shoulders. He looked her over, up and down, following every curve of her body smirking the whole time. She felt dirty and didn't know what to do, she was on her own here, and there was no way she could overpower him. He slipped his hand inside her lab coat and slid it up her hip, onto her waist, and then under her shirt. Dr Strauss was licking his lips as he moved his hand up her athletic frame and onto her bra, which concealed her firm young breasts. She was now panicking, and she wanted this to end. Every time she struggled, he gripped her shoulder more tightly, making her wince in pain. Rosie couldn't speak; no noise would come from her mouth when she tried to scream. The horror in her mind started to spiral out of control, and she began to feel faint, maybe if she passed out, she wouldn't remember what happened. Being a virgin, Rosie didn't want it to be taken away from her like this, from a pervy older man, Rosie had wished for better things to happen. She had never felt so helpless in all her life, the look in the doctor's eyes terrified her.

Suddenly from behind came a voice.

"Oh, hell, no."

There was a loud clonk, and Dr Strauss dropped to the floor like a sack of potatoes. Standing behind him was Benjamin holding a weapon. Rosie jumped over Dr Strauss and immediately hugged Ben bursting into tears. Ben reciprocated the hug and gave the doctor a kick in the head.

"Sick fuck, I knew he was weird," said Ben

"Thanks, Ben, I didn't know what to do," said Rosie between sobs

"What's going on," Tom said joining the party

"This asshole was touching up my sister, so I knocked him out."

"Nice job," said Tom

Tom and Ben picked up the unconscious doctor and dragged him over to the elevator, followed by a sobbing Rosie. They went to the fifth deck and chucked him into one of the cells. The doctor made a grunting noise as he hit the floor.

"Think you'll be in there for a while doc," said Tom

Tom turned and hugged Rosie, she pushed away at first but conceded in the end. She trusted Tom implicitly, but she was still shaken up from her ordeal.

On the bridge there was a lot of discussion about what to do with Dr Strauss, Rachel had mentioned the incident at the reduction room, Dr Franks told them of more than a few episodes at the hanger. They decided that he would stay locked up for the time being, and Jillian would go down with Tom and check on him shortly. Rachel was devastated that this had happened to Rosie, and Cameron was quite rightly furious. They took Rosie back to the sleeping quarters and got her into bed, Jillian had given her some sleeping pills to take so she could rest. She asked for Ben to stay with her while she slept as she felt safe with him around, Rachel and Cameron agreed that would be best.

Dr Strauss awoke on the cold floor of one of the cells on the fifth deck. His head was pounding and was tender to the touch at the back. Touching the sore spot, he felt dampness, and when he moved his hand away, there was blood on his fingers. He sat up and looked around, taking in his surroundings. He realised what he'd done to be locked up, but it was worth it in his mind. Rosie was quite the pretty girl, and being alone all these years with only Dr Franks to look at had made him desperate. His advances towards her had ended up in several kicks to the groin area, which put him off sex for quite a while until he had healed correctly at least. The stock of movies they had on board lacked as well. If the others knew the real reason he left Germany, they would kick him off the ship for sure. Dr Peach and Major Tom appeared at the bars on the cell.

"Dr Strauss, Jillian, would like to check your head if possible." said Tom.

"Of course," Dr. Strauss replied.

Dr Strauss back up to the bars so Jillian could inspect his wound. She cleaned it up with an antiseptic wipe and put a small dressing on it. Dr Strauss moved away from the bars and turned to face them.

"How long do you intend to keep me in here?" he asked

"For now, we don't know, but it is going to be a while. It's hard enough dealing with being in outer space, let alone dealing with a sexual predator." Tom Replied.

"You can't keep me here forever, you know," Dr Strauss replied with a smirk, "You'll need me sooner or later."

"Don't be so sure, Dr Strauss," Jillian said with a spit of venom in her voice.

Tom checked the lock on the cell door and then turned to leave with Jillian. He looked back at Dr Strauss and said

"You're lucky it was Ben that found you and not me."

They both boarded the elevator. As the doors slid shut, they both kept their eyes on Dr Strauss. Once they had gone, Dr Strauss checked his pockets. He soon found the keys he was looking for on the inside of his lab coat sewn into the lining. What the group had failed to think of was the fact that Dr Strauss had designed and built this ship. He knew it inside out, and he knew how to open all the doors. Dr Strauss had sewn the keys into his lining just in case this happened. He didn't trust the rest of the crew, and they didn't trust him. He put his arm through the bars and reached around to the lock, placing the key into the hole. One-click to the left, and the cell door was open.

On the second deck, the group had assembled for their evening meal. Since coming back to the Goon, they had all welcomed the proper food they could have. Rosie and Ben had tried almost everything the ship had to offer and loved all of it. Favourites were cheeseburgers and ice cream, but then that was to be expected, what teenager wouldn't like that. Rachel and Cameron found themselves having to say no to their kids and make sure they had some fruit and vegetables. Tonight's offering was spaghetti bolognese; everyone was a fan of that.

"Tom, you had better take a portion down to Dr Strauss," said Jillian.

"Fuck him," Rachel snapped.

"I agree, but we are not animals," Jillian added.

Tom plated up a portion of the bolognese and headed for the elevator. He stepped inside and pushed the button for the fifth deck. Tom arrived at the fifth deck, and the elevator door slid open. He walked through the armoury and headed for the cells. Arriving at Dr Strauss's, Tom instantly noticed the cell door wide open and dropped the plate of food. Turning on his heel, he headed for the armoury to see if any weapons had gone. Tom found that one Berreta had gone missing along with some extra clips. He grabbed an assault rifle and two magazines, he then attached them to an ammo belt and threw it over his shoulder. Tom ran for the elevator colliding with the door as it slid open. He pressed the button for the second deck and returned to the communal area in the living quarters.

"Dr Strauss is gone," Tom said between breaths. "Don't know where he is."

They all looked at each other, shock showing on their faces.

CHAPTER 17 – DR STRAUSS

Mission Date 380

A few days had passed since Dr Strauss escaped, and they had not seen him anywhere. Several patrols of the ship had turned up evidence of him being around, but he was extremely good at hiding. Rosie hadn't taken the news of the doctors escape very well. Ben was still trying to get her out of her room. He had been teaching her some self-defence in case of him finding her. It was going well, and she was very much the fighter, just like her brother. Ben was currently tempting Rosie with picking some bananas in the Bio-dome. She finally conceded, and they were off to the elevator.

Tom and Jillian had found some alone time and were making the most of it in their sleeping quarters. They were still very much in love and were currently in the middle of some wild sexual acts. It involved some strawberries from the Bio-dome and some whipped cream from storage that Tom had earlier this week. Jillian was in the height of ecstasy right now, and she felt as if she was having an out of body experience. They were both naked, slippery with sweat thrusting into each other, getting faster and faster. Tom was shattered and wasn't sure how much longer he could keep this up, but he was not going to give up.

Rachel, Cameron, David, and the scientists were on the bridge looking at viable planets to land on. So far, they had discovered numerous planets but were looking one with an apparent breathable atmosphere. They were trying to figure out how to use the long-range scanners on the ship, but without Dr Strauss, they were struggling.

Rosie placed her hand on the scanner to enter the Biodome, and the doors slid open. Ben followed her into the airlock, and they awaited decontamination. Inside the Bio-dome, they walked across to the banana trees, and Rosie took a seat. Peeling a banana and eating the inside brought an instant smile to Rosie's face, she did love bananas. Tom stood facing her and also eating the long yellow fruit grinning ear to ear. From behind him, a figure appeared and raised an arm in the air. The raised arm came down fast and struck Ben on the head with a metallic object knocking him out. Rosie froze and started to panic internally. She was staring directly at Dr Strauss.

"Here we are again young lady," said Dr Strauss

Dr Strauss grabbed Rosie by the arm, pulling her up off the floor. Rosie was so terrified she had distanced herself from the situation and disappeared to a place inside herself. Rosie was in the Biodome sat under the banana tree peeling a banana. She was alone, peaceful, all she could hear was the insects buzzing around the flowers. Dr Strauss pulled her out of the airlock and out of the Bio-dome. He forced her into the elevator and pushed the button for the sixth deck. The doors opened slowly on the sixth floor revealing the garage and workshops, dark and silent. He pulled Rosie from the lift and dragged her across to the APC in the garage. Throwing Her to the floor, he stepped on her stomach, holding her pinned to the floor and opened the rear hatch. Inside the APC, there were blankets and food stockpiled with bottles of water. It was like a makeshift campervan inside. Rosie slowly came back from her distant place and soon realised this was where Dr Strauss had been hiding. He Pushed her into the APC and made her lay on his makeshift bed. She began to panic again. She had never felt so small and insignificant, Dr Strauss made her feel so week.

Ben awoke drowsy and disorientated, and his head was pounding. He got up and stumbled forward, grabbing the tree for balance. Ben looked around to see where Rosie was. When he couldn't find her, his heart began to pound uncontrollably in his chest. He remembered what happened with Dr Strauss and a cold sweat started to break out of him. Sweat started coming out of every pore and ran down his back between his shoulder blades. He instinctively ran for the elevator and slid sideways on his feet to the inside. He pressed the button for the bridge, and the doors slid shut.

On the flight deck, the excitement in the room was palpable. Dr Franks, Dr Heals, Cameron, Rachel, Julia and David were all standing looking out the viewing screen. On the display was a blue and green planet very similar looking to earth. Landmasses spread in large green sections across the surface, with vast seas between them. The scanners on the ship had indicated that it had a breathable atmosphere. The hope was to land the spaceship on the planet and explore it. First, they had to figure out how to land on the surface.

The door to the elevator slid open, and Ben stumbled out onto the floor trying to stay on his feet. There was blood on the back of his head trickling down his neck like strawberry sauce on ice cream. Rachel ran over to him and instantly started making a fuss of him. She raised his head to her and asked.

"Ben, whats happened?"

"Rosie, she's been taken by Dr Strauss" he replied, short of breath.

"That's it he's done," said Cameron. "Where's Tom?"

Cameron exited the elevator on the second deck and briskly headed for Tom's quarters. He knocked on the door and repeatedly pressed the buzzer outside several times. Tom opened the door abruptly in a bedsheet and looked pretty angry. His hair was a mess, and he looked totally out of breath.

"What Cameron?" growled Tom

"Dr Strauss has got Rosie," Cameron replied.

"Fuck me, alright I'm coming" he replied

Tom left the door open and darted inside to get dressed. Jillian emerged from the bedroom, naked and confused. She looked directly at Cameron almost unaware that's she had on no clothes. Cameron couldn't help but look at her. He saw the shape of her chest and the curve down her waist to her hips. She was stunning, athletic like Rachel but with a larger bust. Her long red hair flowed down her back like a rippling red river. Jillian's body's showered in freckles from head to toe, and she had milkiest white skin. It made her freckles stand out on her face and arms. As Cameron followed her body downwards, he couldn't help but notice the small triangle of red pubic hair between the top of her long white legs. Cameron found himself getting aroused and had to look away, that's when Jillian realised her nakedness and darted back in the bedroom. Tom came running out of the bedroom, dressed and clutching his gun.

"Enjoying the view?" Tom asked winking as he passed him. "C'mon"

They entered the lift, stopping before pressing a button.

"Which floor?" Tom asked

"I have no idea, where would he have been hiding?" said, Cameron

"I checked all the floors of the ship. I found nothing."

"Where else could he hide, it would have to be somewhere where we wouldn't notice."

"I didn't check the vehicles in the garage."

"The APC!!" they both said in unison.

Tom bashed the button for the sixth deck, and the doors slid shut. Before the doors closed fully, Jillian appeared in the hallway. Tom called out to her.

"Tell the others, the sixth floor."

The doors slid closed, and the elevator descended to the sixth floor. When the doors opened, they both stepped out slowly and quietly. As they crept towards the APC, the doors slid shut behind them, making that start trek noise. Dr Strauss stopped and looked out the windscreen of the APC. He could see Tom Reid and Cameron Hill walking cautiously towards the APC, both brandishing a rifle. He looked down at Rosie. She was on her back, head tilted to her left, staring into space. She was limp and distant, not even aware of Dr Strauss straddled over her half-naked form. Her jacket was open, exposing her bra and small breasts. Dr Strauss had one hand on her chest, and his other was supporting him. Dr Strauss got up and dragged her to her feet. He led her out of the APC and pushed her towards the centre of the garage area. He had a knife from the kitchens pressed to her neck. Dr Staruss was holding Rosie in front of him like a human shield.

"You need me, so there's nothing you can do to me," he said to Tom and Cameron

"You're going nowhere Strauss" called Tom

"Let her go you sick fuck" shouted Cameron

Dr Strauss pressed the knife harder into Rosie's neck drawing blood. Rosie didn't flinch; she was in total shock and had disappeared to a safe place in her mind. Behind Tom and Cameron, the lift doors slid open to reveal Ben and Rachel, both armed. A look of horror appeared on their faces when they saw the scene in front of them. Ben stepped between Tom and Cameron and spoke to Dr Strauss.

"What do you want us to do?" he asked

"I want the others gone, back in the elevator and gone" Dr Strauss replied, "This is between you, this young lady and me. I owe you for this lump on my head. If they don't leave, I'll slit her throat and throw her body out the cargo bay door."

Ben turned and gestured for the others to leave. Rachel shook her head, but Ben nodded and gestured again. He mouthed the words "I got this" and turned back to face Dr Strauss. Tom, Rachel and Cameron reluctantly retreated to the elevator guns trained Him. Tom pressed the button for the fifth deck, and up the elevator went.

"We can't just leave them there alone," said Rachel

"If I know Ben, he's got an idea," said Tom "A crazy idea!"

Ben stood unarmed facing Strauss and Rosie, and he looked directly at Rosie. Her coat and shirt were open, flashing her bra and athletic body. He called to her.

"Rosie come back to us, remember what I taught you."
Rosie twitched and looked into Ben's eyes, understanding in hers. Dr Strauss was still holding her hostage, and she could now feel the knife and winced under the pain. Rosie knew what Ben was implying and remembered the self-defence he and Tom showed her. She stamped her left heel hard on Dr Strauss's left foot, swung her head back and obliterated his nose, grabbed his crotch and

twisted as hard as she could. Dr Strauss screamed in agony and dropped the knife on the floor with a clatter.

Rosie ran straight to Ben, who grabbed her and led her to the elevator. On the way, he pressed the release for the cargo bay doors and sirens began to wail. They got in the lift and watched as the door lowered showing the blackness of space outside. Various tools and boxes flew towards the opening flying past Dr Strauss who was on hands and knees holding a luggage tie-down. He looked up at them and started shouting obscenities in german. A large crate began to move towards Dr Strauss, it flipped and barrelled straight into him, sending out of the open cargo bay door. The lift doors slid shut and stabilised the atmosphere for Ben and Rosie.

On the bridge, David noticed the cargo bay door was open and pressed the remote console to close it. The door shut slowly and sealed with a clunk, returning the garage to normal. Out the viewport, he noticed a frozen angry-looking figure floating in space in a white lab coat.

"Dr Strauss?" he said aloud

Dr Franks turned to see the frozen corpse drift past the window slowly and stiff. She extended her right arm and gave the doctor the finger, satisfying her hatred for him.

Ben and Rosie went up to the fifth deck and met up with their parents. Rachel put her arms around Rosie and held her close. Tom and Cameron both shook Ben's hand and then embraced one another.

"Where's Strauss?" asked Tom

"He's gone outside for a little walk" replied Rosie noticeably pleased with herself.

"Probably looking for his balls too," said Ben with a laugh.

CHAPTER 18 – FEELING THE LOVE

Mission date 395

They had been circling the planet for fifteen days now. Dr Franks and Dr Heals were trying to determine if it was safe to land on the planet. Deciding how to land was hard enough, knowing if they would survive on the planet was another matter. So far, they had learned that there were several seas and three large land masses or continents. They were unable to determine if there was any life on the planet, but they could tell that there was breathable air.

"We could pass through the atmosphere and then scope out the planet," said David from the captain's chair.

"We don't know how the ship will react to the stress of re-entry, it should be fine as it exited our earth's atmosphere with no problem, but we don't know what this planet's atmosphere is like." said Dr Franks.

"We need to have a group meeting and decide what our next move is" Tom replied.

The group assembled on the second deck in the main canteen. Since the exit of Dr Strauss, the mood on the ship had lifted considerably, and Rosie was nearly back to her old self. She had spent most of her time in the Biodome. Even more time with Ben and Tom in the armoury, she was becoming quite the fighter now. They all sat with mugs of tea around the large dining table in the canteen, talking amongst one another. David entered the restaurant from the direction of his quarters. He stood at the end of the table, ready to address the group.

"We are safe enough for the next couple of years to carry on travelling on the ship. We have, however, found a suitable planet for us to land on, though it may be a one-way trip. We currently have no way of knowing if the ship will make it through the atmosphere or even if it will land. We also don't know for sure until we land if the atmosphere is breathable. I suggest we take a vote, do we stay on the ship or land and see what the planet has to offer."

"I think we need to get off this ship for a while," said Cameron

"We're safe up here though aren't we?" asked Rachel

"It's been over a year now, I'm surprised some of us haven't lost the plot," Tom added.

"We vote now," said David "Those who want to investigate the planet raise your hands."

David looked at them all in turn, raising his hand first. They all raised their hand except Julia Hoffman.

"I'm not sure it's been a strange time. I'm not sure I can handle more changes." Julia said, "But I suppose its nine against one so yes, let's investigate the planet."

She raised her hand in agreement, and they all smiled at one another.

"Right into the atmosphere we go" announced David "Batten down the hatches and stow away the beer we're heading into the unknown."

Tom and Ben headed down to the garage to secure all the vehicles and weapons. They took particular care on securing the fuel canisters. Rosie and Jillian secured the medical suites while Rachel and Cameron secured the labs. David and Julia had returned to the bridge to prepare for their descent. They had arranged to all meet on the flight deck in four hours to begin the decline to the planet.

David had decided to leave the bridge for a while and left Julia in charge. He headed to the canteen for a drink to clear his head. All the planning and decision making had given him a headache. He bent to the under-counter fridge and looked through the shelves for a beer. He could hear footsteps coming up to the counter behind him and looked under his arm to see who it was. It was Dr Franks, Abigail, and she was walking right up to him. He looked back into the fridge; he was now looking for two beers. Abigail put her arms around David's waist and gave him a seductive squeeze. She then moved her hands down to his crotch and rubbed his package slowly. David stood upright and turned to face her, and she was smiling at him through sultry eyes. Abigail moved closer to him and rubbed herself against him, kissing his neck. David grabbed her shoulders and kissed her passionately on the mouth.

They began pulling at each other's clothes and kissing more and more intensely. Abigail broke from David's caress and walked up to the counter, bending over it. She slowly slid down her trousers and panties and lifted her bottom into the air. Abigail looked slowly back at David and smiled at him, nodding slightly. David feverishly undid his trousers and dropped them to his ankles along with his boxers. His member already hardened for action, he approached Abigail and slid inside slowly pushing his hands up her back under her shirt. They thrust and pounded each other for several minutes before jointly exploding in ecstasy and sinking to the floor. Abigail looked into David's eyes.

"I wanted to do that in case we didn't get a chance," she said softly

"I've wanted you since we met you know" he replied

"I know, as you can see the feeling is mutual" she whispered in his ear

David looked around the room and across to the table, he noticed a person sat there.

"Not you two now as well," said Ben from the table

"Oh my" laughed Abigail pulling her trousers up

Julia came into the room and spotted David and Abigail in their states of undress. She eyed David curiously and shrugged.

"Fuck's sake, it's like a porno movie on this ship" Julia barked

"Wonder who's going to be next?" said Ben moving up beside her.

Julia looked at Ben and admired the man he had become. He was fit, muscular and very handsome. She pondered being with him and realised the only other free man on the ship was Dr Heals, who was openly gay. Besides, Ben was a real catch, and that would make her a MILF too. She reached out and took Ben's hand and then leant over to whisper in his ear.

"Think it should be you and me next, don't you?"

Ben shook a little nervously but automatically felt some movement in his pants. He was excited and being a virgin; he couldn't help but want this to happen ASAP. Ben could tell she was serious by the way she was squeezing his hand. He smiled nervously at her, not knowing what to do next. She leant over again and whispered in his ear.

"My quarters fifteen minutes."

Julia left the room and headed for her quarters, patting Ben on the backside as she left working her hips. David walked up to Ben, buttoning up his trousers, he put an arm around Bens shoulders and said.

"Go for it, Ben. There are no other options out here."

Rachel and Cameron were on the bridge, waiting for everyone to arrive to begin their descent. They had been in the Biodome most of the day, reminiscing on days past and eating their fill of the fresh fruit on offer. Most of the crew spent time in the Biodome it reminded them of earth. Multiple places from home in one place. Like the jungle, the rain forest and even apple trees like in somerset. Rachel was talking about Rosie and how devastated she was with what had happened to her. Cameron was also distraught with the events of the last few weeks, but he was incredibly proud of Rosie for getting through it.

"Rosie seems so much stronger now. She has been through hell, and it toughened her up a lot. I didn't want that to happen, but I'm glad she is OK." Rachel said

"I don't think she'll ever get over it. As long as she deals with it and doesn't let it ruin her future". said, Cameron

"What future has she got out here, we're not getting any younger hun and when we're dead what happens then."

David and Abigail entered the bridge from the elevator and headed over to their seats. David gave Cameron a nod as he passed, indicating it was time to start the descent to the planet. Abigail took her position at the communications console. David took the captains chair and began prepping the ship. Tom and Jillian entered the bridge together, hugged and then separated to their posts. All of them were now frantically pressing buttons and manipulating the ships many functions.

Dr Heals was on the medical deck, helping Rosie secure the hospital beds and medical equipment. They were discussing the crew and who had paired up.

"What about you, Steven, who do you like?" Rosie asked sheepishly

"It's not a question of who I like, its that there's no one compatible with me. Besides Tom and Jillian, Rachel and Cameron, David and Abigail are all couples, so that leaves Ben and Julia and you. I don't think Ben is my type, do you?" Steven Replied,

"So you like men instead of women then?"

"That's right. I suppose growing up in the wilds as you did, it's hard for you to understand."

"I get it you like guys, I know what being gay is."

"I'm not so sure you do. Anyway, we need to get to the bridge."

Dr Heals and Rosie headed for the elevator and stepped inside. Rosie pressed the button for the bridge and up they went. They both exited the elevator and headed for their seats. Rosie touched her mother's shoulder as she passed, giving a small smile.

"Where's Ben and Julia?" asked Rachel

"Give them a few minutes they'll need it" replied David smirking

"What do you mean David?" Cameron asked

"You know what I mean, Ben's becoming a man," David said with a wink.

In Julia's quarters, she was lying on the bed in her panties, breasts on full display. Ben was stood at the foot of the bed, taking in the view. He was naked except for his boxers. He had a rather large tent pitched inside his underwear which was twitching ever so slightly.

"Why don't you come over here and let me show you how to use that" Julia said in a low voice

"O, O, OK" Ben stammered

He moved on to the bed and moved between her legs. Julia pulled down his boxers and gently caressed his crotch, rubbing his member. Ben shook and groaned and then ejaculated all over Julia's breasts, covering them in beads of warm white liquid.

"Sorry. Julia, I don't know what happened"

"It's OK, Ben. It's what I expected from a strapping young man like you. Let's see if we can't go for round two."

Julia began rubbing his crotch again, bringing it back to life in seconds, more substantial and harder than before. She pulled him closer and planted a kiss on his lips, pushing her tongue into his mouth and searching inside. Ben moved in closer to her feeling her breasts on his chest. He felt the material of her panties against his penis, soft and comfortable. Julia began to grind against him driving his senses wild with every movement of her body. She pulled her panties to one side and guided Ben into her, holding him back, so it went in slowly. The sheer size of Bens penis was a shock to Julia and nearly tipped her to orgasm straight away. Once Ben was entirely inside her, they began to move in unison, subconsciously knowing what each other wanted. They worked together for several minutes until they both came close to climax. Julia stopped Ben and pushed him off her turning herself over and raising her backside towards his crotch. Ben pushed himself back inside her and began to thrust into her. He started slowly and began picking up speed. After five minutes they were both at the peak of pleasure and Ben pushed hard inside, making Julisa scream with pleasure. They both climaxed at the same time, Ben filling her up with warmth that dribbled out onto the bed. They bothy rolled onto the bed and tried to catch their breath while holding each other's hand tightly.

"That was awesome" Ben remarked

"It surely was, better than I expected. We're doing that again Ben." Julia replied, "You're a man now, Benjamin." she added

They laid there for at least twenty minutes before Julia realised they would be needed to be on the bridge now. She rolled on top of Ben and planted a kiss on his lips. Ben could feel her breasts on his chest again and started to get hard. Julia smiled and rubbed it gently.

"Later, my love, later."

She rolled off of him and stood by the bed, her ample bosom wobbly seductively at Ben. She bent down and pulled on her trousers and found a T-shirt in her closet. Ben got up and got dressed, glancing intermittently at Julia getting dressed. She knew this, and every so often made sure he got a glimpse of her breasts and bottom while she got dressed. Together they left her quarters and headed for the elevator.

The elevator arrived at the bridge, and the doors slid open. Ben and Julia exited the elevator together. There was a noticeable spring in their step and a look of guilt on their faces. They both walked onto the bridge towards their posts, aware that everyone was watching them. They split after sharing a short kiss and headed for their stations. Ben and Julia took their seats and waited for their instructions from David. There was a long awkward pause. Julia was grinning ear to ear, and Ben was getting a little nervous. He turned to look at everyone with a questionable look on his face.

"What?" he asked

"Nice!" David replied with a huge smile and a big thumbs up.

They burst into fits of laughter. Everyone was feeling the love in the room. Not just a crew or a team, they were friends and family.

"OK, Julia prepare for descent, start the engines and take us in" ordered David.

" Aye captain" she replied.

CHAPTER 19 – A NEW HOME?

Mission date 395

The ship descended towards the planet circling clockwise. It dipped into the atmosphere shuddering slightly but otherwise running true, almost like turbulence on a flight to sunny Spain. They were descending at a shallow angle being cautious not to put any undue strain on the ship. Like exiting the earth's atmosphere, the ship handled it well. After a few minutes, they broke through the atmosphere of the planet with a jolt and settled out gliding effortlessly through the sky. On the viewscreen, clouds started to form in front of the ship; the colours were astounding. There were purples, pinks and reds like candy floss in the sky. The ship continued and pushed through the clouds breaking out into a vibrant blue sky over lush green lands with mountain ranges and what looked like forests. A sky so blue it almost looked fake, almost like it was animated. The ship glided over the land formations looking for somewhere to set down safely. On the viewscreen, they could see a flat clearing on one of the continents, perfect for landing the craft. As they grew closer to their target, they noticed there were buildings on the horizon. Cities and towns scattered the horizon in front of them. Birds were swooping back and forth, trying to get a look at the alien ship in their sky. This planet was inhabited but by what?

"Julia lets set it down in that clearing," said David

"Yes, captain."

Julia positioned the ship over the clearing and began descending to the surface of the planet. A little shakily the ship grew closer to ground, in anticipation, they all began clutching the arms of their chairs. Leaning forward and gritting their teeth, the ship touched down with a small thud. They all breathed a sigh of relief and relaxed back into their chairs. They were finally on land again after well over a year of travelling through space.

"So, it looks like we may get some company when we leave the ship," said David pointing at the viewscreen.

On the viewscreen, a crowd was gathering outside of the ship. The planet's inhabitants were humanoid not much different from us. Slightly different in skin colour and by all accounts free from any hair. The most curious thing was they appeared to be the same physical size as the crew.

"Let's head down to the cargo deck and see what it's like out there" David instructed

"According to the ship's sensors the air should be breathable for us," Jillian said

They all made their way to the elevator and descended to the sixth deck. They stopped at the cargo door, and David turned to address the group.

"We have no way of being one hundred percent sure that the air is breathable to us out there. I think we should take the chance. Otherwise, we could end up stuck on this ship for the rest of our lives. I'm willing to take the risk, but I think we should vote. All in favour, please raise your hand."

All of them raised their hands at once. Not one of them wanted to miss out on meeting a new race. Plus cabin fever was setting in on the ship, and some fresh air to breath would be a welcome sight. David pressed the button for the cargo door, it hissed and began to drop open, revealing the bright sunshine outside. It took a few minutes for the door to open fully. Once the door was open, they made their way down the ramp to greet the natives. At the bottom of the ramp, Cameron began to feel a little light-headed but shook it off with the excitement of meeting a new people.

The inhabitants of the planet were nearly the same as they were. Their faces were symmetrical and almost perfect like the faces of angels. Their skin was a light purple with no imperfections at all. They all had pale yellow eyes and no hair between them. They wore futuristic-looking overalls in a range of colours. At the front of the congregation was a slightly taller male that looked to be senior or in charge. Gender was evident as they had very similar body type to us; the women had curvy hips and breasts, the men were stocky and muscular. Their leader began to speak in a language that none of the crew understood; he seemed to be welcoming them and gesturing them to follow.

"Hello people, I am captain David Beckett, and this is my crew. We have travelled far and are pleased to meet all of you. I am sorry we do not understand your language."

Cameron was waiting for the 'We come in peace, take us to your leader' speech, but it never came. He just sniggered to himself and caught an annoyed glance from Rachel. The leader was still trying to communicate with them, but he was getting nowhere. David was getting a little frustrated at this point but was keeping his cool for now.

Rosie grabbed Cameron's arm and looked up at him before fainting and falling to the ground. One by one, the crew began to pass out and fall to the floor, except Tom who stood as long as he could. Tom could feel the air in his lungs but knew there was not enough oxygen in it. He realised quickly that they were all struggling to breathe, but it was too late to get back in the ship. He also felt overwhelmed and felt giddy. In a few moments, Tom fell to the floor and passed out.

Tom awoke in a hospital room, bright lights overhead, and he was on a hospital type bed. He wasn't sure what was going on; he felt confused and tired. His eyes were blurry, and his mind was fuzzy. He started to remember the mission, the reduction and getting lost in the wilderness. It felt like a distant dream or memory. He couldn't decide. There was a shuffling noise next to him which made him jump and turn to face a person. Not an average person though, it looked like its skin was purple. Memories started to flood back to him, the Goon, Dr Strauss and the planet they found. He sat up in bed panting trying to speak but coughing when he did. The being next to him touched him trying to calm him, it spoke.

"Please calm down you're alright, you just need to get used to our atmosphere that is all. I am Delak I have been looking after you all. You are in your medical suite on your ship."

"How can I understand you?" Tom asked

"Yes you have a lot of questions I'm sure, when the others awake we will answer them all now lie back and rest," Delak replied

Tom did as he was asked and led back down on the bed. He still felt drowsy and began to snooze and drift away.

They all met on the bridge, talking amongst themselves and discussing what had happened. There was some confusion as it seemed like the crew had all been asleep for several days according to the ships logs. The leader from the day they landed came up in the elevator and entered the bridge, smiling as he walked among the crew and his people. They were all quiet in anticipation of what he had to say.

"On behalf of our civilisation, I would like to welcome you to our planet, Denarion. We are excited to meet new life from the stars. I am Krelak, and you are probably wondering how we can understand each other right now and how you had survived since the unfortunate incident when we first met. Although we too breathe oxygen, we don't need as much as you do. It has taken a total of fourteen of your earth days to acclimatise you to our atmosphere. When you all fainted, we moved you into your medical bay so you could breathe your oxygen-rich air and recover. While you were all sleeping, we took the liberty of learning about you from your ship. We accessed your computers and learned your language and learned about your planet. I hope we haven't overstepped any boundaries, but it was essential to be able to communicate with you and to know how to treat you. We developed tiny, what you would call robots, many years ago, and we have used them to translate your earth language. We have injected them into each of you, and they will be your translators and will help your body to adjust to our planet. Delak is a doctor and will be available to tend to any problems you may face. I suggest you stay on board your ship tonight to adjust and recuperate.

There will be plenty of time to explore tomorrow, Delak will stay with to make sure there are no problems."

The crew had numerous questions they wanted to ask, but they accepted the advice to stay on the ship for today. They all felt tired and still slightly breathless so took the time to rest in their quarters.

CHAPTER 20 – DENARION

Mission date 396

Ben awoke to someone nuzzling into his chest; it was Julia. He couldn't help but smile at the beautiful older women next to him in bed. He took in her curves under the white cotton sheet, noticing her ample breasts and feeling a little twitch in his boxers. Julia stirred and lifted herself on her elbows.

"Morning stud, ready to explore our surroundings, looks like you may want to stay in bed a little longer though" she winked and ran a hand over his package.

Ben smiled and kissed her on the lips as they both laid back into the bed. Julia climbed on top and reached into his boxers, easing him into her as she began to grind on top of him.

Cameron was already up and dressed, pacing in the kitchen. Rachel stretched out as she awoke and noticed she was alone. Rachel sat up and looked around the room, seeing Cameron's clothes were gone. She got up and wandered into the lounge area and saw Cameron in the kitchen. Rachel walked up behind him and put her arms around him, hugging him from behind. She knew Cameron was anxious to explore the planet and to talk to the Denarions.

"Shall we make our way to the bridge and meet the others?" asked Rachel

"Yes let's get going, I have so many questions," he replied

"I know you do Hunny, just try to contain your excitement," she said, turning him around.

Cameron pulled her close and kissed her, squeezing her around the waist and holding her close to him.

"I love you" he whispered in her ear.

Tom and Jillian were in the elevator heading for the bridge, neither of them had slept much. The excitement of meeting an alien race was too much for them. Tom was holding Julia's hand as they exited the elevator. On the bridge, David, Abigail and Dr Heals were looking out the viewport window at the planet before them. Tom and Jillian joined them to take in the fantastic view. David looked down at the two of them hand in hand and smiled at them with a slight nod. Tom nodded back in acknowledgement.

Through the viewport, they could see the buildings in the distance. The buildings were dome-shaped and in groups of five or six. Some of the structures were more significant than others. It looked like a city before them surrounded by lush woodlands and vibrant green fields. The coloured clouds in the sky were magnificent, making it look like a dream world of candyfloss clouds. Behind them, Ben, Julia, Cameron and Rachel came out of the elevator and joined them to take in the view. All of them were in awe of the sight before them. The only word to describe what they were seeing was beautiful.

Delak arrived on the bridge accompanied by Rosie. She joined her shipmates as they turned to greet him.

"I would like to invite you to join me on a tour of our city. The Denarions there are expecting you, so there will be no surprises." said Delak addressing the group. "If you would please follow me down to your cargo deck we can exit the ship and meet the transport waiting outside."

Delak headed for the elevator with the crew in tow like an excited group of school kids on a school trip. They all managed to fit in the lift with a squeeze, and Tom pressed the button for the cargo deck. It was silent in the elevator as they were all unsure what to say. Delak was almost glowing in the dim lighting, which made them feel a little uneasy but not enough to stop them going. There was a strange squeak that came from the centre of the lift, followed by a rather obnoxious smell. They all held their noses and looked at one another in disgust. Dr Heals put his hand up and said.

"I'm sorry that was me. I'm a little nervous."

All of them burst into laughter along with Delak, who also

saw the funny side. It broke the awkward silence and put everybody at ease. The doors to the elevator slid open, and they all piled out quickly to get the fresh air in the cargo bay. Dr Heals was noticeably red in the face and did his best to hide his shame.

The cargo bay door was already open, and they could see an eight-wheeled vehicle outside. Delak beckoned them to follow him towards the vehicle. They all complied and entered the vehicle one by one. He told them it was called an Avantor and this would be like a taxi to us on earth. It was open top with rows of seats facing forward and no driver form what they could see. Delak punched in some code into the front console, and the vehicle began to move. It headed in the direction of the city, gaining speed slowly. Delak stood at the front and addressed them.

"We are heading to the capital city here on Denarion. It is called Garnak and is home to two hundred of our people. It is the city that you can see in the distance" Delak pointed in the direction of the accumulation of buildings. "We have taken the liberty of providing you with somewhere to stay and will give you a tour of the city."

Cameron raised his hand to speak.

"Will we meet your leaders?"

"We have set up a conference for this afternoon to discuss your visit and what happens next" Delak replied.

The journey only took about ten minutes through the woodland and grassy fields. They arrived at a square in the centre of the city, surrounded by domed buildings and market type stalls. Delak led them to a group of smaller domed buildings to show them where they would be staying tonight. The apartments were modest in size with a living/bedroom with what looked to be a bathroom of some kind. There were six rooms in total, allowing the couples to share and Rosie and Dr Heals to have a place each. The rooms were a pale beige colour, the ceilings inside shape mimicking the dome roof. Inside the domiciles felt like the inside of a hut on Tatooine in Star Wars.

Outside the sun was setting behind the tree line making the trees glow amber and the sky wash with multiple shades of yellow. Delak was waiting at the low wall at the front of the apartments. Rosie came out of her apartment first and greeted Delak at the gap in the small perimeter wall. She was mesmerised by the city in front of her, keen to see what it had to offer. Delak stood stiffly, waiting to meet her gaze.

"Delak, this is a beautiful city you have here. I'm looking forward to exploring it," she said softly

"I am going to give you all a short tour of or beloved city" Delak replied, smiling.

Tom and Jillian emerged next closely followed by Ben and Julia. They were all now in the street outside of the apartments taking in the beautiful scenery. The others joined them within a few minutes uniting with them in the street outside. Delak stood in front of them like a tour guide, and they stood like a group of Japanese tourists.

"I'm going to guide you through our capital city. I'll walk you through town and back to our great hall," he stated and turned to face the city.

Delak led them down the familiar-looking streets to the market in the square. The city reminded them all of Cairo. The buildings, the roads, the housing was all eerily familiar to them. It was a beautiful place, and the people were very accommodating, greeting them as they passed. Not one person gave them a strange look or a frown.

The market consisted of wooden canopied stalls selling everything from foods and drink to locally made clothing. Delak introduced them to some of the strange-looking fruits on offer. There were some strange shapes and colours, but they tasted fantastic. Rosie and Ben couldn't get enough of them. Their sweetness was something they had never experienced before. Some of the local meats on offer were good too. Lots of meats that tasted similar to pork were on offer. The men especially enjoyed this. It was the closest thing they had tasted to bacon in years. All it needed was some brown sauce or ketchup depending on your preference. The clothing was mainly like cloak like and an off white colour. Some of the hand made bags were terrific, hand-stitched with multiple colours. They all received a cloth bag each on their journey through the market.

Delak led them on towards the great hall. On the way, he pointed out the education centre of which they were very proud. They could see the children playing in the fields adjacent to the school. The children were playing a game similar to football, a cross between soccer and rugby. The sounds of the children cheering and laughing warmed their hearts and reminded them of home.

CHAPTER 21 – THE GREAT HALL

Mission date 396

As they approached what Delak called 'The Great Hall' They could help but notice that it was in the dead centre of the city. The hall was an imposing sight and overshadowed most of the other buildings. It looked like an Arabian palace with its towers and domed rooves. There were multiple windows in the building and judging by the rows, and it would seem that the building was four stories high.

Leading up to the entrance were a series of deep steps which looked too big for the people using them. They were double the depth of a standard tread. They made their way to the top eventually and stopped for a breather.

"This is our great hall. It is the centre of our world and is where we make all the decisions for the community. It is a great honour to be able to enter the hall, and you have that honour this evening. The Great Hall was the first building we constructed, and we have expanded outwards ever since." Delak explained, standing in front of the massive doors. "We will now enter and take our places for the feast."

Delak struck the doors three times, making a loud booming echo inside. The left door slowly opened, and Delak beckoned for the others to follow him inside. Inside the hall, long tables stood in three rows with stools placed alongside them. There was a sea of light purple beings sat at the tables and stood around the perimeter of the room. At what looked to be the head table were twelve empty seats. Delka headed in the direction of the empty slots and the others followed him obediently.

The feast began with the ringing of a large square bell. Once struck platters of hot food came into the room in trains of steaming plates. The dishes laid out for every four people, followed by jugs of what looked to be wine. They used clay-like plates and tumblers but ate with their hands like the planet's inhabitants. The feast was fantastic, hot meat that tasted and looked like chicken, fresh vegetables, followed by the fruits they had all sampled at the market.

"That was so good" Ben whispered to Rosie

Delak looked at Ben and shook his head, warning him not to speak during the meal. Ben nodded an apology and drank some of the wine. The wine was fruity and fragrant tasting more like a mixed squash than a wine. Still Ben didn't complain, it was about the best drink he had ever had. Once all had finished eating and drinking the bell was rung again. The train of servers returned to remove the used plates and cups and to take the platters of food away. David watched as the leftover food disappeared and wished he could eat more.

At their table, Krelak stood up from the centre seat. He banged a wooden pole on the table three times and began to address everyone.

"We welcome our visitors to our home and hope you are happy here during your stay. We have learned much from you and your computers and would like your help in accessing the outer space as you call it. We do not have the technology you have or the resources to build a ship. We would be honoured if you would take one of our people when you leave us. This Denarion would research and document his journey in an attempt to bring back technology to help us explore the outer reaches of space."

Cameron raised his hand to stop Krelak talking.

"Why do we have to leave your planet sir?" he asked

"Unfortunately, your time here will be short. Our atmosphere is unsuitable for you and will slowly deteriorate your bodies until death. Though we both breath oxygen, there is not enough to sustain you here. There are also some other gasses un-known to you that will harm you. We suggest you leave tomor-row to safeguard you against any long-lasting effects. Delak will be the one to travel with you and document his journey for us."

"Why didn't you tell us before?" asked Jillian

"We were unsure until now, the robots injected into you have reported back deterioration in your lungs already and too much time spent here will cause permanent damage. We are very sorry."

This information automatically put a damper on the crew's mood. The team all lowered their heads in disappointment at this news. They were quite happy to stay here and felt it would make a great new home for them. The team would spend the night here tonight but would have to leave tomorrow. The highs of this morning seemed distant now, and the celebrations they had an-ticipated were now irrelevant.

That evening in their quarters, the outlook was bleak. In the morning they would have to return to the ship and prepare for launch. The crew sat in the back garden area of the apartments. David looked around at his team one at a time, noticing their dis-appointment. He stood and decided to address them all.

"We may have to leave this place but remember, we found an alien civilisation, no one else form our planet can say that. Sure we cant tell them, but we found this planet, so that makes two civilizations including our own. We are not alone in the universe, so that must mean there will be other inhabited planets to visit. We can find a new home I'm sure of it."

"You're correct, Captain. We should celebrate this find and look for the next one. We must find new civilisations, and we have the tools to do it. It should be our new mission" Cameron said, ex-citedly jumping to his feet.

"Now we need to celebrate this and drink more of their wine!" Tom exclaimed

No sooner as he had said that, Delak appeared in the garden with them holding a crate of what looked to be bottles of some-thing. He placed it on the ground in between them and pulled out a metal tool from in his overalls.

"How about we share some of our more adult beverages," Delak said, removing a cork-like object from one of the bottles.

He filled a tumbler with some of the dark red liquid and passed it to Cameron, then continued to fill more cups one by one and handed them out to the others. Once they all had a drink, he raised his own in the sky. The others mimicked him and raised theirs.

"To new friends and new beginnings," he proclaimed.

Delak downed the drink in his hand, made a sour face and then smiled at them. The crew all looked at each other, unsure whether to drink the liquid. Judging by Delak's expression, it was enough to put them off. David shrugged and downed the drink in one, shuddering after swallowing it. The others followed suit, some coughing, some shivering. It tasted like a fruity whiskey and was pretty good by all accounts.

"What is this Delak?" Cameron asked

"Scumpshak. A bit like what you would call whiskey" he replied

They had told stories, laughed and joked and got to know Delak a lot better. The Denarians were not much different to humans other than their looks. There was no religion and didn't seem to be any different nationalities. There were one race and one community. The crew couldn't help but be a little envious of their way of life. No wars, no religious conflicts and everyone worked together. It would've made a satisfactory home for the crew of the Goon.

Several drinks later they were all a bit worse for wear. Drunk would have been an understatement. They were all nearly passed out, so they decided to turn in. It was an excellent way to finish off the evening, but the possibility of a massive hangover in the morning was an unwelcome thought. Once back in their apartments, it wasn't long until they were all asleep.

CHAPTER 22 – THE JOURNEY CONTINUES

Mission date 397

The crew were back on the ship. The team had woken early with no ill effects of the evenings drinking. They met Delak at the Avantour which was waiting outside the apartments. All of stopped to admire the city one last time but couldn't help but feel dryness in their lungs and shortness of breath.

The ride over on the Avantor was quiet and solemn. Though they had found a new civilisation, they were unable to stay and explore it. The team was also exhausted and needed to breathe the healthy air on the ship. Delak was with them, and he too was sad to be leaving his home. He had explained that he could breathe our atmosphere after acclimatizing himself on the ship for two weeks.

On the bridge the crew was picking up again, they felt fit and healthy and were doing checks on the ship's systems. The breathable air in the ship had helped tremendously, and they accepted they had to leave. Krelak had come aboard to wish them well and had brought supplies into the cargo deck.

"I have had food supplies, weapons and some of our technology loaded onto your ship. You may find some of it useful. Delak will know what to do with it all. I wish you luck on your travels and hope we meet again in the future."

Krelak shook all of their hands in turn and pressed his forehead to Delak to say goodbye. He entered the lift and headed down to the cargo deck and out of the ship. David took his seat in the captain's chair and gave the order to close the cargo door. One by one they all strapped into the seats on the bridge, Delak taking Dr Strauss's place. Outside the ship, the Denarions were gathered waving their goodbyes and awaiting the departure of the vessel. The vessel rose slowly towards the heavens spiralling anti-clockwise as it did. This launch they took considerably more carefully than when they left earth. As they ascended, the ground below shrunk away until it was a green blob in a sea of blue. There were fewer clouds as they neared the edge of the atmosphere of the planet, breaking through with little turbulence and settling out in the darkness of space.

The ship was orbiting planet Denarion while the crew took stock of the supplies they had received. In the cargo hold, there were numerous crates of equipment stacked in rows, Delak and Tom were taking inventory. Delak was explaining what was brought aboard and showing Tom some of the contents of the crates. There were six crates of what looked like rifles, according to Delak they packed quite the punch. There were eight crates of materials, wood and metals in manageable lengths. To the right were what Delak described as medicines and medical supplies. To the left were thirty containers of food and water. Delak showed Tom the way they kept them fresh with an ingenious liquid suspension which stopped anything getting at it. Tom described it as being similar to cryogenically freezing something. With the stock take complete, they both headed for the elevator and up to the bridge. Tom was quite excited at firing off one of those rifles but was advised not to do so in the ship by Delak.

On the flight deck, David and Julia were discussing the crew's roles and had decided to give everyone a title and job on the ship, thus giving them purpose. There were some discussions and disagreements, but ultimately they had eventually agreed. They decided they would get everyone together to give out their roles at dinner tonight in the communal canteen.

Dinner time came at seven pm ship time. The crew gathered in the restaurant and took a seat at the large table. There was an apparent nervousness in the team. The crew were unsure what this meeting was about, what was so important?

"Right, Julia and I have been discussing everyone's roles on the ship and have come up with a structure," David announced.

Everyone started to look at each other, more than a little confused.

"So the following, read by Julia, will be the new crew structure." David continued

"David Beckett, Ship's Captain

Julia Hoffman, Chief Officer and second in command

Tom Reid, Weapons Officer

Jillian Peach, Ship's Doctor

Cameron Hill, Science Officer

Rachel Hill, Science Officer

Abigail Franks, Navigation Officer

Steven Heals, Chief Engineer

Ben Hill, Petty Officer

Rosie Hill, Ship's Nurse

Delak, Science Officer"

"Your roles are all equally important and will need to be followed to maintain the future of this ship. Do we have any questions?" added David, there was a silent pause "No, then let's eat."

The crew were happy with their roles and responsibilities. It gave them the purpose which they were lacking. It helped with being stuck out in the vastness of space, the isolation and the impending realisation that they were never going home. They sat around the table idly chatting and laughing, eating the spread of food from earth and Denarion. Denarion food was certainly different to look at but tasted amazing. Rosie sat with Delak, and the two of them were getting very friendly. Ben had noticed this, and although at first, he was a little disgusted, he was pleased for Rosie.

The evening went into the early hours of the morning, and the crew began pairing off to their quarters. Cameron and Rachel headed to their room, holding hands and sharing a kiss on the way. Tom and Jillian head for his quarters, arms around one another. David and Abigail now shared quarters and were getting quite handsy on the way to it. Julia stood up and grabbed Ben's arm dragging him off the chair and proceeded to grope his ass. She chased him to her room, slapping him on the backside a few times. That left Dr Heals, Delak and Rosie at the table.

"Don't mind me it's time for my bed" said Dr Heals getting up from the table

He staggered and disappeared towards his room, a little drunk and worse for wear. Rosie was laughing at the sight of Steven and how silly he was when drunk. The laughing from Rosie amused Delak, and it made him smile at her. She got up and took Delak's hand leading him away from the table. She led Delak to her quarters, stopping at the door. She stood in front of Delak and was looking at him curiously. Rosie lifted herself on her tiptoes and planted a small sweet kiss on his lips. It surprised Delak, so much so he stumbled back a bit. She giggled at this and smiled brightly, proud of herself.

"Good night Delak" Rosie said

She turned from him and entered her room, looking at him while she closed the door. Rosie then ran and dived onto her bed, spinning over, so she landed face up. The bedclothes flicking up in the air as she bounced and settled, looking at the ceiling. She was grinning uncontrollably, happiness bubbling throughout her body.

Delak was a little confused but also felt a warmness inside that he had never felt before. He turned on his heels and headed towards his room but stopped at the door. He felt something drawing him away. Delak headed for the elevator and went inside, pushing the button for the bridge. Arriving at the bridge, he walked over directly to the viewport and looked down at his planet below. He was going to miss his home. He knew he might never see it again; the journey ahead of them was too far to return. Given the fact that the planet's resources are running so low, he knew that his people would be gone soon. Even if he did return, it would be to an empty planet. His whole civilisation had decided to stay, Delak had been the only one to volunteer to go. He had always been slightly different from his colleagues, more into science than their belief system. A small tear trickled down his cheekbone and eventually dripped off his chin on to his chest. He was going to miss his people but felt honoured to take their memory with him on this epic journey.

Morning came fast to all of the crew, by six am ship time, they were all on the bridge at their stations. After several pre-travel checks, they were ready to leave Denarion's orbit and embark on their adventure.

"So Dr Delak where would you like to go?" said David spinning his chair to face him

"I'd like to leave this system and see what others lie in the outer reaches" Delak replied

"Perfect, heading anyone?" David said

"That way," said Rosie pointing at a planet with beautiful multicoloured rings.

"Well, in the words of a famous starship Captain, make it so number one," David said grinning.

There was a long awkward pause until Julia realised he meant her. She fired up the ships nuclear engines, and they moved off in the direction of the ringed planet.

The end .... or maybe it was the beginning?

Printed in Great Britain
by Amazon